HUNTING
THE DARK IMMORTAL

MacLeod froze, feeling . . . yes. Another Immortal was nearby.

And he has to be aware of me, too.

He hurried around the corner, to see a tall, shadowy figure tense, head up, looking this way and that, trying to locate the enemy.

That has to be Khyan!

Just then, a second, smaller man nearly collided with Khyan, presumably apologized, then began unlocking a door. Khyan grabbed him and all but hurled his captive inside. MacLeod raced forward, reached the slammed door, and threw it open—only to be confronted by a wall of nearly total darkness.

There! The thinnest trace of light . . . they were moving up an elevator . . . heading for the roof. MacLeod took a hasty step forward and nearly fell over a body just inside the doorway: a security guard, uniform sticky with blood and throat quickly cut by Khyan.

He was _____ roof before Khyan

ALSO IN THE HIGHLANDER SERIES

Available from
WARNER ASPECT

HIGHLANDER™

THE CAPTIVE SOUL

A NOVEL BY JOSEPHA SHERMAN

ASPECT®

WARNER BOOKS

A Time Warner Company

WARNER BOOKS EDITION

Cover design by Don Puckey
Digital imaging by Franco Accornero

Warner Books, Inc.
1271 Avenue of the Americas
New York, NY 10020

Visit our Web site at
http://warnerbooks.com

🆆 A Time Warner Company

Printed in the United States of America

First Printing: August 1998

10 9 8 7 6 5 4 3 2 1

ACKNOWLEDGMENTS

Thanks go to: Betsy Mitchell, Editor-in-Chief of Warner Aspect, for letting me play in the HIGHLANDER world; Eleanor Wood, Agent Deluxe, for understanding why I wanted to play in the HIGHLANDER world; the HIGHLANDER staff and writers, for creating the wonderfully complex character that is Methos; actor Peter Wingfield, for so beautifully bringing Methos to life; and Admiral Ahmose of Egypt's Eighteenth Dynasty, for leaving first-hand accounts of crucial battle scenes that made this writer's job a good deal easier.

ACKNOWLEDGMENTS

Chapter One

New York City, Riverside Park: The Present

All night he wandered the streets of the garish, noisy island the natives called Manhattan, not sure exactly where he was, what streets, what neighborhoods, save that he was moving ever nearer to the Great River, that which the natives named the Hudson, hunting as he had hunted for many nights.

Again and yet again, he was dazzled by the brightness of the artificial lights turning the good, proper darkness to a never-natural mockery of daylight. Again and yet again, he was stunned by the never-ending flow of traffic. So many lives crowded in together on this island, so many souls. . . .

The hunt was hopeless.

No, and no again! He would not let himself despair. Despair was the refuge of the weak, the commoner. His brother had told him that many years ago, and he believed it, believed his brother . . .

His brother, whom he would find and rescue. No matter how long it took. No matter how many sacrifices must be made. (But . . . how long had he been hunting? There were large gaps in his memory when he must have been doing something . . . living somehow . . . yet he could not remember.)

No matter. Prior sacrifices had told him to search here within this vast city; they had brought him here, up through a tortuous route involving many false words and documents. But now . . .

There. That man, walking alone into the park caught between the river and the wild way, the West Side Highway, the man walking with music blaring and earphones blocking out sounds of the world around him: foolish, foolish. His race, his appearance meant nothing. But the man was so young, so full of careless life—perfect.

He stalked the young prey through garishly lit fields growing ever less crowded, glad of the fact because he knew the hunt must be made in private. He knew that these common lives must not know who walked in their midst, not yet.

He stalked, seeing a perfect place shrouded with trees and bushes, half hidden in shadow, a "shortcut" the young man had decided to take, no doubt confident in his youth and strength, never knowing he was being followed, never knowing that the one who followed was battle-trained and hardened.

Now.

He struck, catching the prey around the throat, cutting off any outcry. Now, now, the first part of the Triple Sacrifice, the rope looped about the neck, all but strangling the Chosen One.

Then, even as life began leaving the choking body, he performed the second ritual, his knife stabbing swiftly up to the Chosen One's heart. Deftly avoiding the spurting blood, he let the dying sacrifice slide to the ground. The earphones had fallen free, and faint, tinny music accompanied him.

Now, yes, now for the third, the final ritual of slaying. . . . His blade rose, fell, severing the victim's head with one swift blow. More blood spurted, coppery-sharp in his nostrils as he knelt by the body. His hands shaking with hope, he tore and cut aside clothing till the body lay uncovered to the night.

He forced himself to calmness, murmuring the proper prayers. But all the time he was thinking, yes, yes, this time the prayers would be granted. Knife in hand, he neatly sliced flesh open, ignoring the new reeks, warily examining organ after organ, reciting:

> "Open to me, oh Light, open to me.
> Let me see truth, let me see truly.
> Let me see—"

Nothing! There was nothing to be read in the size or shape of the organs, not the slightest hint of an omen to be had! The sacrifice had failed once more!

Staggering to his feet, dimly aware of the tinny music continuing, incongruously cheerful, he stumbled blindly away, wiping his hands clean on a scrap of cloth. He must not be found with the sacrifice, he knew that much, or even leave the cloth behind, not in this strange, strange city where such things as sacrifices were not allowed and clues could be taken from a mere drop of blood.

He must not be taken. He would not let himself be cast into captivity like some hopeless slave!

Hopeless. As soon as he was at a safe distance, away from the park and its too-bright lights, hidden in the shadows of an alleyway, he sank once more to his knees. Of course the ritual had not worked. He was no priest or sorcerer!

Burying his face in his hands, he huddled there, weeping for his lost, lost brother.

But this was not safe, either. Predators prowled this city, those who hunted any weakness, predators who just might chance on the one true way of slaying. He could not die before his goal was reached, could not lose his soul until his brother's soul was freed.

So be it. The sacrifice had not worked because it was not meant to work. The gods had not forsaken him; they merely tested him, as they had done and done and done—

He must not question. He must try again, closer this time to the water, the sacred, flowing water. . . . He would try again, and yet again, as often as he must. There were endless victims to be found in this teeming New York City. And at last, at last, he vowed, he would succeed.

Determined anew, he sheathed his blade and set out into the night.

Chapter Two

Duncan MacLeod, in perfect New York style in his casual black blazer, white shirt, and black trousers, his dark hair caught back in a neatly groomed ponytail, stood on the northeast corner of Fifth Avenue and Seventy-first Street on this sunny May morning, ignoring the never-ending roar of traffic and enjoying the new day's warmth. It had only just turned ten o'clock; he had a few minutes to spare. With not a sign or feel of danger anywhere, MacLeod smiled and allowed himself the luxury of a few peaceful moments of just playing tourist. Why not? He'd come to New York to check out an important estate sale, had even found a handsome mid-nineteenth century writing desk almost worth the inflated price. But today he was free to answer an invitation.

On the far side of Fifth Avenue, Central Park was lush with spring greenery and noisy with school groups on their way to visit the Children's Zoo a few blocks south. He was standing on the more commercial side of the avenue, with row after row of expensive offices and apartment houses. The Branson Collection, there on the south side of Seventy-first Street, was a charming anachronism, a Victorian mansion full of the stone eccentricities of the period and masquerading as an eighteenth-century Italian villa complete with central garden.

MacLeod could remember the building from an earlier era. Edmund Branson, shipping magnate, had held many a glittering party in that mansion a hundred years ago. Gaslight had glowed from the marble walls back then—no new-fangled electricity to spoil the effect, thank you very much—and there had been the soft rustle of satin gowns and murmurings of pleasant conversation. Outside, the only sounds of traffic had been the clopping of horses' hooves and the roll of carriage wheels.

The unromantic *blat* of a bus horn shook him back to the present. New York, MacLeod thought with a wry smile, had never been a city for any Immortal seeking stability. It didn't merely change every century; it redesigned itself every few years!

He crossed Seventy-first Street, dodging a taxi and a group of giggling, admiring teenage girls, and entered through the ornately carved stone doorway of what was now not a magnate's home but a small museum still owned by the family, as well as the site of the Branson Foundation offices.

He stopped in the small, marble-walled lobby, getting his bearings. The space had definitely been rearranged yet again. To one side was a mahogany desk labeled INFORMATION, staffed by an earnest young man who was probably an art student, and beside it was the predictable rack of postcards. But beyond that, three corridors, one of them still with the fresh paint scent, led off into the building.

Before he could ask for directions, a shrill voice called, "Duncan? Duncan MacLeod? It *is* you!"

A balding, scrawny little man was scurrying toward him down one of the older hallways, grinning widely, and after a second memory triggered the right name.

Amazing. Even after a decade or so, Professor Albert Maxwell still looked exactly like one of those small, friendly, nervous little terriers that are never still for a moment.

"Professor Maxwell," MacLeod said solemnly.

The professor was clutching a newspaper and several

manila folders in his arms. After a moment of awkwardly shuffling items, he managed to get a hand free, and MacLeod, fighting not to laugh, shook it.

Maxwell didn't let go. "Welcome to the Branson Collection!" Shake. "So glad you could make it!" Shake, shake. "It's been . . . how long since we've seen each other?" Shake. "Ten years?"

MacLeod gently pulled his hand free. "Something like that."

Staring up at him, Maxwell *tsk*ed. "Amazing, simply amazing. You don't look a day older, while I . . ." He ran a hand self-consciously through his thinning hair. "How *do* you do it?"

"Clean living," MacLeod told him dryly.

Maxwell laughed. "Good genetics, too, I'd say, yes, and all that nice, clean Pacific Northwest air."

But then the professor stopped short, blinking. "Ah. It's a bit late now, but I, uh, never did get a chance to offer face-to-face condolences. . . ."

An unexpected pang of grief stabbed through MacLeod, still surprisingly sharp after all this time since Tessa's death. "Thank you."

But Professor Maxwell wasn't quite ready to let the subject drop. "So terrible, what happens today: random violence, I mean, drug crimes, madmen— Look at this!" He brandished the newspaper almost accusingly in MacLeod's face. "Another of those so-called cult killings, and right here in New York! We do *not* have serial killers in New York!"

Of course not, MacLeod thought wryly. *And that series of serial beheadings back in . . . ah . . . 1985 was just a minor incident.*

MacLeod had heard about the most recent killings; given the media's enthusiasm for gore, it had been impossible *not* to hear about the killings. All had taken place along the Hudson, most in Riverside Park, which had given the media a convenient handle: the West Side Slayer. That the bodies had all been beheaded had given MacLeod a moment's start, but they'd also been carefully disemboweled and laid out according to a definite plan. Not necessarily the work of an Immortal, then. Just as probably a mortal lunatic.

"Random violence," he reminded Maxwell wearily, "is nothing new. Neither, unfortunately, are ritual killings."

"True enough, true enough. 'The more things change,' and all that."

"Indeed," MacLeod said wryly.

"Which brings us to the Hyksos, those, ah, charming folks, and of course you've come to see the Hyksos Exhibition! So nice that you should be in town just now."

"So kind of you to invite me!"

"Yes, well, I thought you'd appreciate it, knowledgeable man that you are. Follow me."

As they walked down the newly painted corridor, passing neatly framed floral prints and charts, their footsteps ringing on smooth stone, Maxwell continued, glancing up from time to time at MacLeod as though making sure he was listening, "Quite a coup for us, the Branson Collection, getting this show when no less a museum than the Metropolitan wanted it. But it was our parent foundation that did the engineering work for the Egyptian government—you know that, I think—yes, and uncovered most of the antiquities in the process, so . . ."

His triumphant sweep of an arm took in the banner proclaiming over an archway: THE HYKSOS: CONQUERORS OF EGYPT. True enough, MacLeod thought, even if their conquest had taken place almost three millennia ago and had lasted less than a hundred years. He smiled inwardly. As Darius might have put it: a mere blink of time!

"Building looks different, doesn't it?" Professor Maxwell crowed. "We put in improved lighting in the last two years, and redivided some of the exhibit halls. Quite a few changes since your first visit, eh?"

If only you knew!

A severe woman in a severely cut business suit hurried up to Professor Maxwell, dipping her head in impatient courtesy to MacLeod, then whispering in Maxwell's ear. He gave MacLeod a stricken glance. "I completely forgot. I'm supposed to be making a conference call just about now. With Management. Would you mind very much . . . ?"

MacLeod solemnly assured the professor that he was quite capable of seeing and, yes, understanding the exhibit all by himself.

"I'll rejoin you later," Maxwell assured him. "We can, as they say nowadays, do lunch. Yes? Splendid!"

Waving Maxwell away with a grin, MacLeod roved the small, circular gallery. Now he knew exactly where he was. This, if his memory was correct, had been Edmund Branson's music room, an imitation of a Roman rotunda, complete with paintings of rather overblown pseudo-Classical deities on the curved ceiling high over-head . . . yes. They were still there, nicely restored and still opulently ugly. The narrow balcony still rimmed that ceiling, too, intended to make a cleaning crew's job easier. MacLeod had once pointed out to Edmund Branson that it would also make any prospective burglars' job easier, too, but had been ignored. Now, electronic alarms or no, the balcony remained.

Amazing that Amanda never discovered it in some nocturnal visit, he thought.

He turned his attention resolutely back to the exhibit. It was nicely mounted, considering the annoying lack of data and some very old-fashioned, wood-framed, glass-box cases: good maps and concise, clearly worded labels explaining the political situation in Egypt circa 1600 B.C. to a lay audience. Not too much was known about the Hyksos, save that they had come out of Palestine but weren't of Hebrew stock, had conquered, then lost Egypt, and had then faded back into obscurity. But the lack of information didn't make them any less interesting for—

MacLeod came abruptly alert, aware in every sense of the sudden blazing presence of another Immortal, a quick protest shooting through his mind, *Not here, not in an art gallery—all these precious, fragile things!*

But then MacLeod relaxed as he recognized the lean figure so casually comfortable in loose gray sweater and jeans stepping out from behind an exhibit case.

"Fancy meeting you here," Methos said coolly. The narrow, sharply planed face had already fallen into its usual enigmatic mask, though humor glinted in his eyes. "Business or pleasure?"

MacLeod shrugged noncommittally. "A bit of both. And you?"

"Oh, I just wanted to see if there was anything here I recognized." Methos being Methos, it was impossible to tell if he was joking. "Not," he added, glancing at a case full of bronze arrowheads, "that the Hyksos were people anyone would want to claim as acquaintances."

"Oh?"

A shrug. "It's rather difficult to like dictatorships, particularly those involved in building an empire by killing off enemies in clever, painful ways."

"Speaking from experience, are we?"

That earned him a sly sideways glance. "That, my young friend, was quite a long time back."

"But?"

"But yes, in the words of the sages: 'Been there, done that.' They were a bloodthirsty lot."

"Nothing new there."

"Why, MacLeod, how cynical!"

"Not cynical, just honest. Civilizations change, but people, good or bad, remain people." Remembering the newspaper that Professor Maxwell had been waving about with such indignation, MacLeod added, making his point, "If you've been following the local news, you know we still have a few psychopaths running around."

"Ah, you mean those garish murders on the West Side, don't you? You're right; I couldn't quite avoid hearing about the West Side Slayer, either, though I've managed to escape the lurid details, thank you very much."

"Turning squeamish, are we?"

"Hardly that." Something dark glinted in Methos's eyes for a fraction of a second. "I just don't find psychotic killers entertaining. We both know how easy it is to kill—how all too easy it can become to enjoy killing."

Then Methos grinned, and the hint of darkness was gone so quickly that MacLeod wondered if he'd imagined it. "One good thing about the Bad Old Days," Methos said, almost lightly. "There might have been just as much general bloodthirstiness, but there was very little in the way of media. You didn't have the Crime of the Day trumpeted into your ears at all times."

"Now who's the cynic?"

"Realist, MacLeod, realist."

They strolled on together, studying the exhibit, both of them pretending by unspoken agreement to be just two ordinary men on a day off. They had the place pretty much to themselves at this early hour on a workday, but MacLeod suspected that there never would be much of a mob. Nothing flashy here, after all: just bits of metal and the potsherds that told archaeologists more about the past than any gold. He remembered from the days of the antique store (flinching away from the intertwined thoughts of Tessa) that only the most knowledgeable of his customers had been drawn to the plain-hilted katanas; the majority had gone straight to the flashy, useless parade swords with the pretty hilts.

Yes, and speaking of swords, here was one beautifully preserved bronze blade. As they both leaned over the case to study it, MacLeod caught the reflection of Methos's face—which had suddenly gone closed and mysterious.

"I never thought I'd see *that* again." It was barely more than a whisper. "The sword that holds a royal soul."

MacLeod straightened, staring at him in surprise. "The, ah, what?"

"The sword that, as a result of ancient prayers or magic or whatever you want to call it, has a royal soul forever trapped in it."

"You can't possibly believe that!"

Methos straightened with a defensive shrug. "We all believed a great many strange things back then."

"And now?"

"And now," Methos retorted evasively, "as I said, I never expected to see the blade again. It's been safely lost under the desert sands for, what, nearly three thousand years. But now it's been uncovered."

"And?"

A sharp grin. "And scholars are probably delighted. Well? What else did you expect me to say? This *is* the twentieth century, after all."

But for all the grin, Methos's eyes had once again grown shadowed.

Chapter Three

Egypt, Nile Delta: Reign of Pharaoh Sekenenre, 1573 B.C.

Methos stepped off the ship's gangplank onto the soil of Egypt, getting his land legs back and welcoming the blaze of heat and clear, bright light.

Ah yes, Egypt. He took a deep breath. The wind had shifted away from the sea, and the air was dusty and laden with the odors of overheated men and beasts, plus someone's decidedly rancid cooking oil, but it was, above all, blessedly *dry*. After a hundred years or so of wandering in far-off Albion—that island with its good beer, friendly women, intriguing henge monuments, and abysmally chill, dank weather—after a hundred years of that, even this too-fragrant furnace heat was welcome.

It was more than the change in weather. An unwanted flash of memory brought him young Prince Amar back there on Albion, a lonely, brooding youngster Methos had befriended. There'd been a quick-witted intelligence in Amar, and Methos had done his best to help the boy out of his black moods, seeing in him the promise of a noble king—

Then the crops had failed. And Amar's brooding had turned to something . . . suicidal—no, Methos told himself, he would not remember a prince become a willing sacrifice, and his own utter disgust at the waste of a young life. He'd had to leave Albion, or he would have said or done something suicidal himself.

But this was Egypt, a whole different world in itself. Listening to someone playing a thin, intriguingly intricate tune on a reed flute, Methos smiled faintly. He *liked* this land; always had. No morbidity here, no dark, brooding religion. No, there was something very appealing about a people who enjoyed life so much they could think of no happier afterworld than one in which life simply continued as it was. *Without the flies,* Methos added silently, slapping at his neck.

The last time he'd been here, the pharaoh had been Merneferre Ay, probably long dead by now. Methos had done the god-king a favor, solved a political dispute or two, and been given a royal medallion as a reward. Methos let his hand slide down to it, safe in its little leather pouch on the thong about his neck. The medallion was one of the few items he'd bothered keeping over the years.

After all, time moves slowly in Egypt. One never knows when a pharaoh's gift, even from a past pharaoh, might be useful!

A subtle glance about assured him that he was dressed like almost every other man on the dock, which in this hot climate meant underdressed: nothing above the waist save the medallion on its thong, below the waist a lightweight kilt of bleached linen reaching to his knees, and sandals of woven palm fibers on his feet. The only militant touch about him was the bronze sword in its scabbard—but then, other men were armed as well. His features, Methos had learned long ago, could be mistaken for those of almost any Mediterranean race, and a few others as well. There should be no trouble—

Shouldn't there? Methos froze, staring at the expected row of whitewashed mud brick houses—and the unexpected row of stakes before them.

The stakes that each bore a man's head.

Fighting down an Immortal's survival instinct suddenly screaming *Get out of here now, don't ask questions,* since he obviously couldn't jump right back on the ship he'd just left, Methos hunted frantically for a sane, safe explanation.

Criminals, that's all, he decided. *Or maybe there was some local uprising. Nothing worse, surely. Taking heads never was much of an Egyptian custom.*

Most of the heads looked vaguely surprised, he decided, or even resigned—

"You! Just off the Levantine ship—this way!"

Ah. He was being ushered into a line with the other arrivals. Methos took his place without complaint. A hundred years ago, the Egyptians had been big on bureaucracy and, heads on stakes or no, there was no reason for that fact to have changed. That was one of the agreeable things about this Land of Khemt: Minor matters like the reigning pharaoh might change, there might even be the occasional civil uproar (he glanced quickly at those ominous heads)—but Egypt, gods bless its stable heart, went on seemingly forever.

Did it? A crowd of guards was gathered about what was evidently the port official's post—and not one of them looked Egyptian. The same dark eyes and hair as the locals, yes, the same tanned skin, but those heavier features and stocky bodies belonged to some land farther east. Their swords were made of sleek bronze, elegantly designed, finer, Methos thought, than anything made by Egyptian smiths. Had the pharaoh, whichever one might rule in this century, taken to hiring foreign mercenaries?

"Who are those?" he whispered warily to the man behind him.

A glare was his only answer. The man in front whispered over his shoulder, "Hyksos."

Well. That wasn't much information. Still, he would pass through whatever the latest version of port clearance customs might be and get away from here as soon as he—

"All attend!"

That was bellowed out by someone with the leather lungs of a professional crier. "All attend the death of a seditious traitor!"

Methos, caught in the sudden crush of people forced together by the soldiers, thought, *We don't have much choice in the matter!*

"Seditious," someone muttered to his left. "Stupid, that's all."

"Eh?"

"Stupid for speaking truth."

There were frantic *shh*'s about him, the sound of men terrified of being overheard. But the one who'd spoken added, almost in Methos's ear, "Called Prince Khyan touched by the gods."

"Touched by Set, more likely," another daring voice muttered, Set being the closest thing to a demon in the Egyptian pantheon, and there were ripples of nervous laughter.

The ripples stopped as though they'd all been abruptly struck mute. In the sudden, utter silence, two guards dragged a weakly struggling man forward. An ordinary Egyptian, Methos thought, nothing notable about him at all.

Except that he was about to die.

His face white with terror, the man was forced to his knees before a block of stone. One guard raised an ax—even in that moment, an analytical corner of Methos's mind noted its foreign design—then brought it whistling down. Blood fountained from the crumpling body, and the guard, showing no more emotion than one who'd just swatted a fly, held the dripping severed head aloft. The crowd let out its breath in a collective sigh.

I've taken enough heads in my time, Methos mused, *but never with such utter . . . indifference. I don't want to be in a place where they cut off your head so casually!*

"Your name and purpose!" a rough voice barked, and Methos nearly started.

Life went on, and so did the passage through customs. Alarmingly, the customs official, a hard-featured middle-aged man in plain white linen robes, was no Egyptian, either. He bore the same not-quite-right appearance as the guards, and his accent was . . . wrong.

I really must keep up on current events, Methos thought wryly. *I had no idea there'd been an invasion.*

He gave his name, since "Methos" was nicely nonethnically specific, and added with a carefully charming smile, the image of that headless body fresh in his mind, "A visitor."

Bad choice of words. "A vagrant, you mean?" the official sneered, and Methos, instantly summing up the type of man he faced, thought, *Gods curse it.* He had just given this petty autocrat some unexpected sport. "Or can that, perhaps," the official continued, "not be 'vagrant' at all, but . . . *spy?*"

He deliberately raised his voice on that word, and the guards all tightened their hands on their sword hilts.

I suppose it really *wouldn't do any good to show old Merneferre Ay's medallion.*

Silently condemning the official to the desert wastes— no, no, to that still-bloody ax and a clumsy headsman— Methos told him mildly, "Hardly anything so dramatic."

What am I, though? Something nice and safe: nonseditious. Ordinary . . . or maybe not quite ordinary if they behead ordinary folks.

But this stupid, arrogant creature wasn't going to let his newfound toy go so easily; Methos had seen his class of bureaucrat, bored and correspondingly sadistic in a petty way, many times before—though usually not with an executioner lurking in the background.

Ah well, if the wager wasn't safe but you couldn't back out, then go for the wildest throw of the bones.

"I am merely a pilgrim wishing to tour the holy places of this ancient land," Methos said, and almost smiled. Staring directly at the official, he added, "the . . . specially holy places."

He moved a hand in what was intricate enough to have been a magical gesture, and saw the official flinch.

Splendid! "Ah, you understand me!" It was said without

the slightest hint of warmth. "Surely there is no harm in that type of visit?"

A second pseudo-magical gesture: *Am I a sorcerer? Do you dare risk finding out?*

A second flinch.

"And surely," Methos purred, his tone not quite a threat, "an important man like yourself need not waste time on a humble pilgrim?"

Still smiling mysteriously, he made a third pseudo-magical gesture, and the official said hastily, "You have already wasted too much of my time. Move on."

Methos solemnly bowed and obeyed, thinking, *Thank whatever gods there are for superstitious minds!*

But, a bit unnervingly, the official shouted after him, "Do not think to return! The guards and I have marked your face in our memories—and in the records! You have been recorded!"

The perils of a literate society. Methos smiled, showing nothing of his emotions. "I had no intention of returning." *And let that not be an omen.*

Invasion or no, commerce must continue, so he strolled in seemingly perfect calm along the river dock, hunting. Yes, thank whatever Powers there were, here was a granary ship, curved of prow and stern in Egyptian style, bound up the Nile for Memphis, the royal capital, and Methos gladly booked himself passage on it. Nothing luxurious: Sleep on the deck, eat with the crew.

None of whom bore axes or any disconcerting hints of Immortality. Good enough.

There was a strong wind blowing down from the north, as there often was. As soon as the crew had rowed the ship out into the Nile, the rectangular flaxen sail, striped an ornamental tan and black, snapped full, sending the ship surging upriver. Later on, the crew might need to break out the oars again, but for now, both the wind and tide were with them.

Leaning on the rail, watching the vegetation-green and sandy-yellow banks of the Nile move smoothly past under the dazzlingly blue desert sky, thinking that this was very much a land of pure, basic colors, Methos could almost forget those heads on their stakes back in port. Soon enough they'd be in Memphis, and at the capital he should be able to learn—

But it wasn't.

"There's the capital these days," an Egyptian sailor muttered to Methos, and spat. "Avaris."

A hundred years ago, nothing but a small town had inhabited that swampy site. Now it was heavily fortified, with a massive wall of unornamented mud brick, possibly one or even two bowshots thick, set back from the Nile by a flat, level field and broken at regular intervals by square watchtowers. Behind the wall loomed a great war fortress, something utterly foreign to this land, and a canal had been cut from the Nile through the swamp to further isolate the site.

Feeling his way, Methos asked warily, "And the pharaoh rules from there?"

The sailor gave him a contemptuous glance. "You *are* a foreigner! Pharaoh Sekenenre, Whom the Gods Love," he added with a quick, wry gesture of reverence, "rules what he is allowed by our overlords to rule, and holds what court he can down in Thebes. Which, of course, we do not hold license to visit."

That, Methos mused, was not leaving him with many choices. He could hardly return to the Nile delta and hope that the customs official wouldn't remember him before he could find a ship away from Egypt; the man might have been superstitious, but that didn't mean he hadn't written some telltale record as threatened and advised the guards to keep a strong watch for a certain visitor.

On the eastern bank of the Nile were occasional villages, but with nothing but desert beyond them. On the western bank were occasional tombs and even more desert. Striking out across that near-waterless expanse would be suicide—or, Methos thought with a shudder, in the case of an Immortal, multiple suicides. Death by thirst, repeated over and over—

Memphis, then, and, from Memphis, on to Thebes. From there . . . the land of Nubia lay to the south, hardly an ally of Egypt, but hopefully not under Hyksos rule. A quick talker should be able to make his way across Nubia to the coast of the Red Sea and take safe passage from there.

Odd, though, how disappointed he felt.

Methos gave a wry, silent little laugh. He hadn't realized till this moment just how much he'd depended on Egypt being there as it always was, an anchor for an Immortal's wanderings. Equally odd how angry he felt at its loss.

Think how the Egyptians must feel about it! Methos snapped at himself, and asked the sailor, "Are any ships sailing as far as Thebes?"

The sailor eyed him suspiciously. "If you wish to sail there, stranger, you'd better have a Hyksos scroll of safe passage. Otherwise," he added with a shrug, "your best bet is to walk."

Walk.

Ah well, if he followed the Nile, he would come across villages where he could find food and drink in exchange for stories of the outside world. And it wasn't, Methos thought wryly, as though he had any pressing engagements or a scarcity of time.

Walk it would be.

Several days later, Methos sat on the banks of the Nile, resting his feet, watching the never-ending flow of water rippling in the late morning sunlight, and envying the waterbirds riding the currents with seeming ease.

Until a crocodile grabs them. No free rides in this world.

Cynical. But then, he had grown mightily tired of walking, and mightily disheartened by everything he'd seen.

Yes, the pyramids still stood, gleaming in the sun as they had since the long-past days when they'd been built (he had been there for some of that process; amazing how, even with that large workforce, they had moved those great blocks of stone so swiftly); no mere foreign occupation would harm them.

But Memphis, celebrated Memphis, was now but a shadow of its former glory: The Hyksos had sacked it pretty thoroughly during their first invasion a hundred years back, and the city—what was left of it—had clearly never recovered.

And here, too, had stood those grim rows of heads on stakes, warning without words: See the payment for rebellion.

Charming.

Each village Methos had reached after that, going on along up the east bank of the Nile, had been pretty much like the next: small, mud brick houses and tough, wiry, wary villagers, the descendants of untold generations of tough, wiry, wary villagers. Their ancestors had welcomed strangers a hundred years ago, but Hyksos domination had made this generation so suspicious of outsiders that Methos had actually had to flee a few villages or be stoned.

Hyksos, he thought with distaste. *Hikau-khoswet,* to be quite accurate. The word meant "Desert Kings" or "Foreign Princes" or even "Shepherd Kings," depending on who was doing the telling. No one seemed sure exactly who the Hyksos were, other than that they'd come from the east and were tyrants determined to slaughter anyone who didn't submit to them.

Wonderful. Just wonderful.

Egypt: a land with no standing army, no cavalry, no long-range bows—

Why not just hang out a sign reading, "Come Invade Us," and have done with it?

The sun was well above the horizon by now, and the full heat of the desert day was approaching. No one but an idiot challenged it, so Methos found a quiet spot with a rocky overhang to shade him. No one around, nothing venomous to sting or bite him.

So be it. Elsewhere there might be invaders and heads

on stakes. Here, at least for the moment, there was nothing but peace.

His peace shattered in a sudden storm of men's voices. Methos woke with a start, scrambling to his feet, hand on sword hilt, to find that while he'd slept, an army had overwhelmed him—

No, no, not an army: These were Egyptians. And it wasn't surprising that he hadn't heard them approach, since they were all on foot, with most of them wearing not much more than he. A mob, then, of badly armed, foot-weary, but determined men.

"Rejoice!" one of them told him. "You are part of the fight for our freedom!"

"Sorry, but I'm not—"

"Are you not a true-born son of Egypt?" another man cried.

"Well, no, actually—"

A storm of accusing questions whirled around him:

"Do you deny your heritage?"

"Are you a coward?"

"A traitor?"

"A spy?"

"No to all of that," Methos cut in before the crowd's mood could turn dangerous. "I am nothing more or less than a wanderer, and if I happen to look like one of you, believe me, it is merely a chance of—"

But all at once, no one was listening. A tall man, lean-faced and no longer young, had jumped dramatically up on a rock. He was one of the few wearing any sort of armor, a linen tunic overlaid with strips of finely worked leather, and while his leather headdress was far from a formal crown, it was encircled by stylized, protective wings.

If memory serves, only royalty wear those.

No doubt about it. Everyone around him was bowing nearly to the ground. No mere princeling: This could be none other than Pharaoh Sekenenre.

Couldn't stand being a vassal one moment longer? Methos asked him silently.

Sure enough, the pharaoh was proclaiming in grand and ornate style, "This is a just and a holy mission! We, the son and brother of the gods, so decree it! And he who follows Us shall never be forgotten by gods or men! Further . . ."

Methos mentally discarded the rhetoric, which he'd heard in various similar forms over his years in this empire and that kingdom, and waited for the kernel of truth. Ah yes, here it came: the final blow to the pharaoh's tolerance, the final injury to his pride. There had been a recent message from the Hyksos king, Apophis, contemptuously bidding Sekenenre to silence his hippopotamuses, since their constant empty noise kept Apophis awake. The message had been couched in the deliberately condescending tone of an adult to a not-quite-bright child.

"We are not mindless beasts or humble slaves!" Sekenenre shouted. "You are all free men, true, honorable men of Khemt, and We, son and brother to the gods, shall lead you to victory!"

To your graves, more likely. "Never mind our lack of an army or superior weaponry, let's go and wipe out the Hyksos!" Thank you, but if I'm going to lose my head, it's not going to be in a hopeless cause.

The others had no such qualms. Methos, glancing about with a cynical lack of surprise, was surrounded by men cheering and shouting like so many idiots.

Nothing like patriotism to wipe out common sense.

He was slapped on the back, nearly knocked off his feet: one big happy band of brothers. That was the trouble with looking like a member of any number of races; these Egyptians were sure he was one of them, and if he tried to argue or to stay behind, they really would think him a traitor or spy.

So be it. He would go along with this makeshift mob till nightfall, one more docile and obedient recruit—then quickly slip away into the darkness. Then, off to Nubia and the safety of the Red Sea. Leave these suicidal patriots to their game.

But a sudden storm of shouts and wild noise sweeping down upon them from the north told Methos that it was already too late for any escape.

Oh, of course, he thought, whipping out his sword. *Everything else has gone wrong, so why not this? Here comes the Hyksos Welcoming Committee.*

And how do I get out of this mess?

Chapter Four

Egypt, Nile Valley: 1573 B.C.

Stupid, Methos thought, parrying a cut from a gleaming bronze blade that would have taken off an arm, staggering back a step as the shock of impact shivered up to his shoulder. *Stupid,* he added, recovering, slashing at his opponent's knees with his own sword, and forcing the man back. *Stupid and stupid!*

It wasn't as though he was some brand-new Immortal without any instincts for survival. It wasn't as though he hadn't had sufficient warning right from the moment he had stepped off that cursed boat onto Egyptian soil.

But no, here he was smack in the middle of a battle that wasn't even his, surrounded by shouting, screaming, dying men and the sickening reek of blood and mortal death. The Egyptians had been utterly unprepared for that damned Hyksos cavalry. Those two-horse chariots, each with one man driving, one man free to fire arrows at will or slash down with his sword, had already made one swift, horrifying charge, smashing the first line of the hastily assembled Egyptian force into so many broken bodies. And as soon as the chariots regrouped—

Ducking right under a sideways slash from a new foe and stabbing up at his belly, opening nothing more than a cut in that cursed bronze-scale and leather armor the Hyksos warrior wore, Methos twisted, turned, got in a good thrust to the enemy's sword arm. Someone else cut the man down, but before Methos could take advantage of the moment's confusion to get out of there, yet another warrior closed with him.

Stupid!

He cut, slashed, cut again, trying to win himself some free space, very much aware that while a brief linen kilt might be suitable everyday attire, it left one woefully unprotected. He'd been cut a dozen times, though never badly, never enough to weaken him, but it was just a matter of time before he suffered genuine injury—maybe even a chance beheading.

No real chance of escape, either, even if he could win free of this crush, not with his back to the Nile: He'd sooner be cut down by a Hyksos sword or arrow, if it came to that (always assuming, of course, that his head stayed attached to his neck), and take his chances about reviving amid the carnage, than die more slowly and painfully in the jaws of a crocodile.

Damn it to whatever gods were listening, here came the Hyksos cavalry for a second charge.

You would think that in a hundred years the Egyptians would have figured out the worth of horses and chariots, but no, they had to go and be traditionalists.

The world suddenly narrowed. He saw only the one chariot, heading straight toward him at full speed, saw the white-rimmed eyes of the maddened horses, one bay, one dun, the red of their distended nostrils, and behind them, the leering charioteer and the archer beside him, bow drawn. No time to get out of the way. If he stabbed at one horse, the other would trample him. But he'd seen a daring escape once in Mesopotamia: onager chariot back then, not horses, but the same idea should work.

Methos leaped to one side, grabbing for the nearest horse's reins, unfortunately just as a body crashed into him—a young man, his startled mind registered in a flash of time, very young, Egyptian, glint of gold, important somebody. The arrow the archer had aimed at him whirred past them both, so close to its target that Methos hissed in pain as it raked his arm. Grateful glance from the Egyptian, who probably thought Methos had deliberately saved his life.

No time to agree or argue—the horses shied, and Methos, altering plans more swiftly than thought, caught the chariot rim as it sped by, nearly jerking an arm from its socket as he left the ground, twisted in midair, and landed in the chariot with a jolt. Too close for the archer to use his bow. A quick sword thrust took care of the archer, and a shove toppled him from the chariot—which was lurching so wildly with the sudden shifts of weight that Methos nearly followed the body overboard. The charioteer, swearing under his breath as he fought his team, couldn't even spare a glance at this intruder.

A second alarming lurch—the young Egyptian, a quick study, had just leaped on as well, his boyish face contorted with warrior rage. Before Methos could stop him, he'd cut the charioteer's throat with a slash of his sword, giving Methos time to think only, *You idiot, he had the reins,* before blood spurted everywhere and the horses, overwhelmed by this hot new horror spattering their backs, bolted.

The reins, dammit, where—

Methos made a frantic snatch for the flapping reins, missed—ha, yes, caught them just before they disappeared over the chariot's rim, all four of them in one swoop. He hastily arranged the set in his hands so that he wouldn't snare a finger and lose it in the process.

Steady now, steady. He'd driven a chariot a time or two in his life, but not for over two hundred years! Still, onager or horse, the mouth was the same, and: *Don't pull the reins too sharply, keep the pull even on both sets of reins . . . there now, they're calming . . . as much as horses can calm in the middle of battle.*

A wailing shout from a dozen throats made him start and glance sharply back over his shoulder.

"The pharaoh!"

"Pharaoh Sekenenre!"

"Oh gods, gods, our pharaoh is slain!"

His young Egyptian passenger cried out in anguish, then grabbed blindly for the reins, struggling with Methos. "The body!" the boy shouted at him. "We must save the body!"

What about our own bodies? In another moment, the young idiot was going to upset the chariot. "Yes!" Methos snapped, since he couldn't get rid of his clinging passenger and there wasn't another choice. "Hold fast to the rim and *don't move!*"

With a shout and a snap of the reins on their rumps, he sent the horses plunging back into the thick of things, into a chaos of shouting men and shrilling horses, dodging arrows, ducking wild blows from sword and mace, thinking that he who saved the pharaoh's body might be a hero, but he who lost his head in the process wouldn't much care.

There! "Get him. Hurry."

The chariot pitched over onto one wheel and Methos quickly threw his weight to the other side: Back on two wheels with a jolt, but—

He hastily leaned the other way as the young Egyptian made a frantic lunge, nearly dumping himself out of the chariot. The sensible thing would have been to shove the youngster all the way out and leave. Instead, not sure why he was bothering, Methos caught the boy's arm with one hand, taking a deathlike grip on the rim with the other.

With a desperate heave, the youngster dumped what Methos hoped was the right body on board.

It had better be the right body! I'm not doing this again!

With another shout and a slap of the reins on the horses' rumps, Methos urged them into a renewed burst of speed.

"Full gallop now," he crooned to them. "Yes, that's right, you brave creatures. Run. When we get somewhere safe, I'll see you both get a good currying and whatever they feed good, swift horses around here. Just keep running!"

All around them, the Egyptian troops were fleeing in total disarray, some of them struggling to stay aboard stolen chariots, others running on foot. If the Hyksos pursued them, they were all dead.

But no pursuit followed.

Why not? They could get us all!

No. The Hyksos commander probably saw no reason to risk his men any further. Logical in a way, Methos thought, slowing his exhausted team to a trot, then a walk. The commander could hardly have taken this disorganized mob for a serious threat. He might not even have known he was fighting a pharaoh; a quick glance at the body's battered head, which had long ago lost its headdress, revealed nothing that proclaimed royal.

Ah yes, and if the Hyksos king allowed even a vassal pharaoh to rule the south, that must mean that he was worried about spreading his own forces too thin. Egypt was big, after all, and the Hyksos probably didn't have enough men to enforce their rule over all of it. Far safer to allow there to be a vassal pharaoh—one with no army—even with the attached occasional risk of rebellion.

Safer as long as you have the superior army, that is.

Which, with their horses, chariots, better bows, and finer swords, the Hyksos undeniably had.

There hadn't been a sound from his passenger—his living passenger, Methos thought dryly—for some time. Worn out from battle and shock?

I could understand that!

Methos gradually brought the horses from a walk to a stop, jumping down from the chariot to see what he could do for the poor, panting beasts. They needed a good rubdown and whatever they fed horses in this part of the world. But for now there wasn't much he could do for them save let them catch their breath, maybe walk them about to keep them from getting chilled after all that exertion. His passenger—

Was silently weeping. Grief for the dead pharaoh? Or was this something more? Something more personal? Suddenly wondering, Methos glanced down at the battered body, up again at his passenger. So, now, interesting. . . .

The boy was somewhere in his late teens, and his face hadn't quite settled into its adult lines—but it bore a definite resemblance to the late Sekenenre.

Now aren't you glad you didn't pitch him out of the chariot?

Should he say something? No. Give the boy a chance to recover his composure.

Which happened in an amazingly short time. Or not so amazing at that, Methos considered, since in his experience few royal fathers and sons were on truly close terms, and most princes were given rigorous upbringings in self-control.

"You are . . . who?" the youngster asked in an autocratic tone, the regal sternness of his face spoiled only by the redness still in his eyes.

"Methos. And I am addressing . . . ?"

But the youngster straightened, looking back over the route they'd taken. "Survivors," he said, and relief was clear in his voice.

Leading the straggling Egyptians was a tall, strongly built young man perhaps a decade or so older than the teen, striding along, for all his disheveled weariness, like a true warrior. And there was something about his face . . . ah yes. Difficult to miss the familiar resemblance.

As if Methos had had any doubts, the man stopped short with a joyous cry of, "Ahmose! Brother—thank the gods!"

He rushed forward to catch the youngster in a fierce embrace. "I couldn't find you—I was afraid—"

But Ahmose—Prince Ahmose, Methos corrected himself—pulled back, face somber. "Kamose, be strong," he said as firmly as though he were the senior, and pointed to their father's body.

"Oh . . . gods . . ."

Methos watched the quick play of emotions across Kamose's face: shock, sorrow, then the dawning of stunned realization. Of ambition. After a few moments, Kamose straightened with new dignity.

But it was Ahmose, his young voice fierce and clear,

pitched to rise easily over the crowd's cries of dismay, who proclaimed, "Hear me, hear the words of Prince Ahmose! Pharaoh Sekenenre has gone to join Osiris and his brother gods! But he has not left us unguarded or alone: All hail the new Son of Horus! All hail the new God-King on Earth! All hail Pharaoh Kamose!"

So now, Methos thought amid the storm of half-hysterical cheering, *I really did rescue someone important! Not merely the son of a dead ruler, but a living pharaoh's own beloved brother.*

That it had been by accident, that at the time he'd been tempted to toss the troublesome boy out on his ear—no. There was, Methos thought dryly, such a thing as being too truthful.

And clever of you, youngster, to take charge so swiftly— and to put the burden of command so squarely on your brother's shoulders.

The newly named Pharaoh Kamose wasted no time. "We cannot show our father's body its proper respect just yet. The rites can only be performed at Thebes. There, we shall have time for—for mourning. Now we must simply survive."

He tallied up the survivors, the wounded, with an efficiency that pleased Methos. "I see," the new pharaoh continued, "that we have captured four Hyksos chariots and their teams. Excellent. The most severely wounded shall ride. The rest of us must walk. But we must make haste!"

"And you?" Prince Ahmose asked Methos sharply.

"Well now, I don't have much of a choice, do I?"

A hint of a similar sardonic humor flickered in the prince's eyes, warning Methos: Young in years or no, this one is no child. "Traveling through Hyksos-held territory *is* out of the question, isn't it?" Ahmose said. "And if you're planning a trip through Nubia—you were, weren't you?—be advised that those traitors are now the Hyksos' allies. No one gets across our southern border these days."

His mouth almost quirked up in a smile, a boy's satisfaction that he'd gotten the better of an adult. "You didn't know that, did you?"

No, Methos most certainly had not known that. "My loyalty," he said dryly, hand closing about his royal medallion, "is all with Egypt."

"I thought it might be."

"Why not? After all, someone has to show your men how to handle the reins."

Ahmose eyed him with sudden skepticism. "You are a charioteer?" he asked doubtfully.

"It's not my primary occupation," Methos agreed. "But believe me, Your Highness, I have been many things in my life. Right now, 'alive' and 'comfortable' are highest on my list of priorities."

That forced a startled little bark of a laugh from the young prince. "And excellent priorities they are. Let us only pray the gods that we achieve them! We shall talk again, my mysterious savior, you and I and my royal brother, when we are safe in Thebes."

"In Thebes," Methos agreed.

When I have more of a chance to decide who and what I shall be.

Chapter Five
===

Egypt, Thebes: Pharaoh Kamose's Reign,
1573 B.C.

It had not, Methos thought, been exactly what one might
call a pleasant ride. Not with the hot desert sun blazing
down on them, and an increasingly less fresh corpse
aboard the chariot with them.

And Thebes . . . well now, someday it might be a mighty
city, but right now it was little more than a very provincial
one. It was larger than most towns, granted, full of two- or
even occasional three-story buildings crowded in together,
but almost all of it was built out of the same plain mud
brick as was used to create those farming villages back
along the Nile.

As the bedraggled troops returned, crowds wild with
disbelief and horror rushed out into the narrow streets to
surround them, staring and weeping, women tearing their
clothes and raking their skin with their nails in frenzied
mourning. Soon all Thebes echoed with lamentations that
grew louder and yet more furious as the dead and living
pharaohs approached the royal palace.

This, at least, was set off from the rest of the city by a
surrounding wall. And here at last, Methos thought, was
some grandeur. Both outer walls and inner buildings had
clean, simple lines that pleased the eye, and were actually
of stone, not mere mud brick. Painted lotus blossoms and
palm trees ornamented their surfaces, the colors bright red,

green, blue, and yellow in the dazzling sunlight, all under that dazzlingly clear turquoise-blue desert sky.

Here in the royal courtyard, the storm of mourning continued unchecked. But Methos noted one figure standing to one side in dignified silence. She was a small, slight woman in a simple gown of white linen, her only ornament a necklace of red and blue beads, but her hair was covered by that blue and gold winged headdress worn only by royalty, and she was flanked by reverent attendants.

The queen, then. No, Methos silently amended, as they approached her and he got a better look. Not the pharaoh's widow, after all: the dowager queen. This was surely one of the oldest mortals he'd met, but there were still echoes of the delicately lovely woman she had been, and her bearing was still proud and assured.

Prince Ahmose, leaping down from the chariot, rushed to her side. "Mother and Wife of the Gods," he began formally, then added more gently, "Grandmother. We have both sad and glorious news."

"My husband's son is dead." It was said with quiet resignation. "The God-King Sekenenre is dead. Did the gods not already warn me and give me time and enough for grief? He is with them now, a god among them. The funeral rites," she added with sudden sharp practicality at sight of the body, "must be brief." A wave of a hand brought servants running. "See to it. And bring my priests to purify this site."

As the late pharaoh's body was taken reverentially away for what embalming could still be performed, the queen's sharpness faded. She added almost vaguely, "And you, my grandson, my Ahmose, are pharaoh."

Ahmose drew back in genuine horror. "The gods avert! Kamose is pharaoh, not I!"

"Ah, of course. I grow confused."

But as the ancient, too-wise glance fell upon Methos, he felt the smallest chill race up his spine. That had not been the mental slip of an aged woman. This mortal had a Gift.

Kamose, if she calls your brother pharaoh, then your

years are running out. And, Methos added uneasily to himself as she continued to study him, unblinking and thoughtful, *I also think she may know something of what I am.*

He bowed deeply as he was introduced to her, this Dowager Queen Teti-sheri, widow of one pharaoh, recently bereaved stepmother of a second pharaoh, grandmother of a third.

A thin, graceful hand beckoned him forward. "My grandsons think me merely an age-crazed old woman," she murmured. "But you, I think, know better."

Methos, feeling his way, said nothing. Teti-sheri nodded as though he'd uttered something profound.

"I wish to speak with you." It was a command. "But later, later. First . . ." Her voice faltered for the first time. "First there must be a proper time for the court and the royal family to mourn. His wife—his widow—Queen Ahhotep, is overseeing our lands to the south; she must be notified. She will not possibly have time enough to reach Thebes before the rites are finished, and the work of holding the southern border safe is far too important for her to leave—but the amenities must, of course be observed."

But then Teti-sheri raised her voice regally. "My grandsons, make this man welcome. He shall, I believe, prove most valuable to you."

He shall prove most valuable to you.

Methos bit back an oath of sheer impatience. A month had passed, ordinarily an eyeblink of time to an Immortal, and yet . . . a month, and—nothing. Not even private quarters, although he'd hardly been treated with discourtesy. And granted, the royal brothers needed time in which to mourn—and time in which a very new pharaoh could begin consolidating his strength.

Patience, he told himself, *patience.* The month had been pleasant enough, in a restricted way. He'd not been allowed out of the palace, nor to speak more than the most casual words to guards or servants, but it had been soothing to sit by a pool, as he was doing now, and do nothing but watch lotus flowers bloom and ornamental fish splash.

Out there in the world this past month, Methos knew, the royal embalmers would have been horribly rushed to mummify what was left of the royal body. *I do not envy them that task!* Royal mourners, professional chanters and singers in their gray gowns, would have followed the mummy across the Nile to the west bank, the Land of the Dead and the site of royal tombs. Surely Sekenenre would have had a suitable resting place prepared long before this; all pharaohs did. And, Egypt being Egypt, no doubt the same prayers and spells would have been said over him in his final resting place as had been said over dead pharaohs for over a millennia.

"You are not departed dead," Methos recited softly from memory, "you are departed alive, to be seated on the throne of Osiris, with your scepter in your hand. . . ."

He couldn't recall the rest. There was something moving, though, about mortals trying desperately to gain their form of immortality.

I did not come here to turn into a—a sage!

A sudden shadow made him turn to see a guard looming over him. "Yes?" Methos asked sharply.

"My pardon for startling you, my lord. You are to appear before Pharaoh Kamose and Prince Ahmose."

At last! "I am most honored," Methos said, and got to his feet.

Of course the royal brothers were going to want to question him fully now that the official period of mourning was ended; of course they were going to be wary of just who they allowed within arm's length.

And still nothing was being accomplished! Here they sat under this cursed awning in this cursed courtyard, going over the same matters yet again, and even though cool drinks sat on a nearby tray, he couldn't take one before Kamose and Ahmose, who showed no sign of wearying.

"Yes," he told them for what was at least the third time,

"my family has, indeed, had a long-standing and quite friendly relationship with your land. And yes, my . . ." a quick mental calculation of mortal generations, "grandfather was given this medallion by the God-King Merneferre Ay for services rendered to the crown."

The brothers exchanged quick glances. Ahmose got to his feet, seemingly disinterested in the proceedings, looking out over the courtyard's central pool with its blazingly white water lilies. "Then you claim to be some manner of ambassador?" he said over his shoulder.

"No." One did not lose one's temper before royalty. Even royalty whose parents hadn't even been conceived the last time he'd visited their land. "I am not an ambassador, a merchant, a spy, or a mercenary. I am merely a traveler who happens to enjoy seeing the world."

The cobra-headed crown of a pharaoh covered Kamose's hair these days, and there was a regal simplicity to the golden pectoral across his chest and the spotless white of his linen kilt. But as he leaned back in his cedarwood chair, fingers steepled, he was all wary warrior. "You speak our language fluently for a foreigner. Almost too fluently."

"Pharaoh Kamose, I speak the tongue of far-off Albion, too, but that hardly makes me a native of that land, either." Methos shrugged. "A man may learn many languages if he lives long enough."

Prince Ahmose turned from where he'd been apparently studying those water lilies in great depth. "And is clever enough."

Methos dipped his head in wry agreement. "And is clever enough." *As you are, youngster. Too clever, in fact, for comfort.* "I repeat, oh God-King, I am not an Egyptian—"

"I believe that," Ahmose cut in, returning to his chair. "Your accent is aristocratic, but all in all rather . . . archaic."

"Hardly surprising," Methos retorted, face a careful blank. "I learned the language rather . . . a long time ago."

That deliberate echo of Ahmose's tone sparked a flash of humor in the young prince's eyes. "If that is so, if you really are new to this land, or newly returned, why were you fighting with us against the Hyksos?"

"It seemed a good idea at the time. Besides, I'm not fond of people trying to kill me."

Ahmose smiled thinly. "In other words, you are wanted by the Hyksos."

Far too clever! Methos's smile was just as thin. "I would hardly put it so strongly. Let us merely say that I don't care to go visiting them." He added flatly, "I don't approve of people who mount other people's heads on stakes."

"Neither," Kamose cut in, "do we."

Methos raised an eyebrow. Neither brother was quite at ease yet, and he exclaimed as though highly indignant, "I am *not* a spy! No Hyksos agent would ever have saved Prince Ahmose's life."

"Ah, then that *was* a deliberate rescue."

In fact, much *too clever.* "Prince Ahmose," Methos said with his most charming smile, "I have already sworn that I am no mercenary. Believe me, at the time I had no idea in all the many hells who you were."

That forced a laugh from both brothers. "I believe him," Kamose said. "No spy would ever be so honest."

"Or so blunt," Ahmose added, eyeing Methos with sly interest. "Deliberate or not, I do thank you for the rescue. And at any rate, we must accept you. Dowager Queen Teti-sheri has so decreed." The warm affection in the boy's voice softened the stark words. "She would speak with you next."

Kamose chuckled. "Our sympathies, Methos. You may find the Hyksos more merciful." He gave Methos a regal wave of a hand. "You have our leave to go."

Queen Teti-sheri was waiting for him, there in the growing twilight, sitting straight-backed and composed of face in her little garden. The only sound was the small splash made by a fish jumping in the pretty pool and the twittering of birds in the interwoven flowering vines that shaded the garden.

She might, Methos thought, have been a ruler, not merely a dowager queen, so proud and elegant she looked, and he, respecting her age and dignity, gave her as courtly a bow as ever he'd learned.

"Flatterer." Her voice was amused. "Come, straighten. You make my back ache watching you. Come, come, approach! Your honor is safe with me, and mine with you. Yes," she added at his startled raise of an eyebrow, "we are genuinely alone. I grant you permission to touch the royal person, Methos. Give me your arm. I would walk about my garden a bit."

"As Your Majesty wishes."

"So formal! I said that we are alone." She glanced sideways at him, her hand a feather's touch on his arm. "They think me a fragile old woman. Well, old I may be, but not fragile, not," Teti-sheri added acerbically, "in mind, at any rate. The gods have given me a Gift whether I like it or not, and I have no choice but to use it."

"True of us all," he murmured.

She glanced at him again. "What? What goes on behind that clever face of yours?"

"I was merely . . . pitying you, Your Majesty."

"Pitying!"

"A Gift such as yours cannot be an easy burden to bear."

"Ah. No. It is not. I foresaw the death of my beloved lord husband, he who was Pharaoh Tao and is now with the gods, and I foresaw the death of my foolhardy stepson, my husband's son. So it is, so it is. And . . . it may be that Ahmose shall, indeed, be pharaoh before he is fully a man—no, say nothing of this to Kamose! It shall not come to pass, I think, for some time yet!"

She paused. "*Now* what are you thinking, oh sly one?"

"If I may speak frankly? Yes? I am wondering what it was you truly wished to say to me."

Teti-sheri stopped short, turning to look up at him. The

twilight softened the lines of her ancient face, making her look so lovely, and so otherworldly, that Methos froze.

"You are not of our kind," the queen said flatly. "No, do not try to deny it! My Gift showed me that from the moment I first set my gaze on you. What you are, I know not. But the gods have sent you, and I can only pray they have sent you to save Egypt."

Oh. "I . . . am only one man, Your Majesty."

"You are from the gods! Bah, and before you think I truly have slid into the madness of age, no, I am not expecting you to—to fly on the wings of the wind to slay King Apophis and banish all the Hyksos just like *that*!"

The snap of her fingers was startlingly loud in the twilight quiet. "Then, Your Majesty, what do you expect?"

Her sigh was soft and weary. "You have traveled far, seen much—more, I have no doubt, than either of my grandsons. You know the weapons the Hyksos use, and you know the way the Hyksos fight."

"Yes."

She stared up at him, unblinking. "Help my grandsons as the gods will it, show them the new ways—these 'horses,' these 'chariots.'" She used the Hyksos terms; there were no equivalent words—yet—in the Egyptian language. "Yes, and they have finer swords and bows, do they not? Oh, don't stare at me like that, I was queen to a pharaoh! My life is more than pretty gardens and handmaidens."

"They do have finer weapons. And horses. And chariots."

"Ah, now I've started you thinking!"

Methos risked a wry little smile. "It is an interesting puzzle, isn't it? I take it that the Hyksos have forbidden the Egyptians the use of the new weaponry?"

"They have."

"An additional problem."

"Ah, but one you must solve. You have no choice, do you, man from the gods? You cannot escape our foes any more than can we."

She was very much Ahmose's grandmother. Methos thought quickly about his only alternative: Living quietly in farming village after village, with absolutely no mental stimulation, no challenges, merely waiting out the years till the current generation died out and no one remembered him . . .

Which, judging from the hale old age of Teti-sheri, might be yet another hundred years. A boring, tedious, sterile hundred years.

And, damn it, he didn't want to leave Egypt as it was now! Illogical to risk himself for those who weren't even his people, but there it was. He wanted *his* Egypt, his safe, unchanging haven, back again.

"No," Methos admitted dryly, "I cannot escape. And, as the saying goes, 'If one cannot flee, one must fight.' But if the odds are overwhelming . . ."

"Sly One, what else?"

Methos smiled slightly and saw an answering wry humor sparkle in her eyes. "If the odds are overwhelming, Your Majesty, why, simply put, there are other means to fight than by force."

"I was correct," Teti-sheri said with satisfaction. "You will, indeed, prove most valuable!"

No, dear queen, keeping my head firmly attached to my shoulders will prove far more valuable. To me, that is!

But he couldn't say that to this gallant old woman. Instead, Methos murmured only, "From your mouth to the gods' ears," and bowed.

Chapter Six

Egypt, Thebes: Reign of Pharaoh Kamose,
1573 B.C.

Methos paused in the doorway to the private room he
had at last been granted, allowing an obsequious servant to
enter first, both because the servant seemed so insistent on
making sure everything was *just right* for this now-
honored guest, and because now that night was here, it was
too dark in there for him to want to enter without knowing
exactly what might lie inside.

At least the room was part of the main building of the
royal palace, an honor in itself, looking out onto one of the
lovely courtyard gardens. And from what he could see in
the dimness past the servant's shoulder, it was large and
freshly swept; Methos sniffed appreciatively at the faint,
fresh scent of cedar. It was pleasantly cool in there now
and would probably prove comfortable even by day, since
the windows, in sensible Egyptian style, were set deliberately high in the walls, just below the ceiling. They would,
he knew from prior experience, allow even the slightest
breeze to circulate.

The servant had been bustling happily about straighten-
ing bed linen and the arrangement of clothes chest and
bedside table, clearly so familiar with the layout he needed
no lamp. But then he paused, glancing back over his shoulder as though only now aware of the guest's discomfort.

"Ah, forgive me, my lord."

With a quick flash of a striking stone, the servant lit an oil lamp, setting it on the table. The room was suddenly bathed in a soft, flickering golden glow that added a glamour to everything—and, more important, revealed nothing perilous. At Methos's wave, the servant gave a quick bow and scurried out.

So, now: home. For the moment. Methos, used to considering such things almost instinctively, noted that the room would be, should it come to that, easily defensible.

Not, of course, that he was expecting any out-and-out treachery from the royal brothers. They had no reason to betray him. It was merely that one did not survive very long by being careless and—

And the room was not empty after all.

"You. Out of the shadows."

"Of course, my lord." It was a silken purr. "You shall not need your sword. Not . . . *that* sword, at any rate."

The woman who moved slowly and gracefully from the shadows was very blatantly bearing no weapons save, Methos thought dryly, those the gods had given her, since her only clothing was a jeweled, fringed belt hanging low on her full hips. He stood bemused, enjoying the sleek golden curves of her: lovely face, small, perfect breasts, narrow waist, the dark mystery below. . . . Long waves of dark hair cascaded down her back, but a stray ringlet curled seductively down over one breast, stirring as she breathed.

If he waited a moment more, he wasn't going to be able to speak at all, so Methos asked, "Who are you? And for that matter, whose?"

"I am Tiaa, lord. And as to whose: yours, my lord."

"A pleasant idea, Tiaa. But who sent you?"

"Why, is that a problem, my lord?" She took a smooth, gracefully swaying step forward, and that distracting ringlet bounced even more distractingly. "I am no slave."

"A free woman may yet have a master. Who sent you?"

"*Tsk,* so insistent. Know that I am the gift of the royal

household to you, for however long you wish. Quite . . . voluntarily on my part, I might add."

There was nothing on her face but anticipation, nothing in her eyes but delighted curiosity: Here was one who clearly enjoyed her work. And clearly royalty was offering him the best. Flattering.

Not unheard of for courteous hosts to offer such hospitality. Also not unheard of for such hospitality to hold a double meaning. At least there wasn't any immediate threat: There was absolutely no place for Tiaa to be hiding a weapon. And the Egyptians, unlike others Methos could have named, had never been ones for such exoticisms as poisoned fingernails.

Immortal or no, there were limits to self-control, and it had been a long, long time since those friendly women of Albion. Even though the ship he'd been on had also put in at Malta, with its fierce, independent females (also friendly enough, when it pleased them), well now, it had been a long time since Malta, too.

"What an excellent idea!" Methos said. Putting the bronze sword aside—but not quite out of reach—he pulled the smiling Tiaa into his embrace and found the bed with an outstretched foot. Difficult to be the gracious host just now: It really *had* been a long time. The jeweled belt went flying, and so did the carved wooden headrest as he and she, Tiaa giggling with delight, fell onto the bed.

And then it was mouth on mouth and hand on silken flesh, it was gasps and moans and cries of joy.

Afterward, Methos knew that he had slept—but slept lightly. Even then, even then, part of his mind had still been wondering. He glanced sideways at Tiaa. Fortunate that the bed was wide enough for two or they would, in that first wild frenzy, have ended up on the floor with the headrest and jewelry.

Ah, but now Tiaa was awake as well, smiling faintly, looking pleased as a cat. Her eyes glinted in the lamplight as she studied him, and her skin was washed with gold.

Methos hoisted himself up on an elbow to look down at her, enjoying the view, and saw her smile widen. She drew her arms languidly back, stretching up at him, like a seductive cat, indeed.

"Again, my lord?"

"Not exactly."

Smiling, he drew one fingertip teasingly across one lovely breast, hearing her gasp as he delicately ringed but didn't quite touch its nipple. Then, before Tiaa could move, he pounced, catching her wrists with his free hand, straddling her, still smiling. Tiaa laughed, deep in her throat.

"Yes, my lord. Do what you will."

"Oh, indeed."

He had learned more than mere survival in those long years. His fingers skillfully stroked that golden skin, caressing till she writhed beneath him. His fingers and lips teasing, toyed, never quite gave release, till Tiaa's laughter turned almost to sobs.

"Now, my lord! Please!"

"First tell me, lovely Tiaa. Tell me who sent you to me."

"I told you!"

"Not enough, my sweet. Who sent you to me, and why?"

She fought him, fought for release, but he allowed her neither. Suddenly Tiaa gasped out a laugh, face gleaming with perspiration and eyes smoky with dark delight. "Oh my sly, sly lord, if you must know, it was the prince, the young prince."

"Ahmose!"

"I am his, and . . . ahhh, and h-he wished to know what you might let slip when . . . when distracted or . . . sleeping or . . . oh yes, yes, my lord!"

Speech was all but impossible for him, too, by this point, but Methos managed, knowing what he said would go soon enough straight to Ahmose's ears, "I say very little. Nothing in betrayal."

Of myself, he added silently.

And then, being after all only flesh and blood, he gave up clear thought for a time more.

Methos stretched, yawning. The hour was unforgivably early, and every muscle was crying to him to stay in bed after last night's exertions. But in a desert climate, the day started early, before the heat set in, and he could already hear people moving about outside.

He had, of course, awakened alone. Tiaa had slipped out long before the first hint of dawn, back to the women's quarters, or more probably straight to Prince Ahmose to report.

What, I wonder, has she told him? Or, he thought wryly, *is that taught him?* No surprise about a boy Ahmose's age—what, mid-teens, maybe?—having a woman or two: Princes in hot climates were often precocious and were expected to be educated in all aspects of life. *At least Ahmose shows signs of excellent taste in . . . the arts.*

The morning was already growing warm. Methos slipped to his feet, stretching again, lithe as a cat himself, not yet bothering to dress, and found the Egyptian version of sanitary facilities—an actual, separate little room, this being a civilized land.

Returning, Methos began the series of smooth, acrobatic exercises he practiced each morning, stretching and relaxing each set of muscles in turn. An Immortal might not have a choice over body type or basic appearance, but if you wanted to go on being an Immortal, you kept yourself fit. Methos had been born with the agile, deceptively lean build of a distance runner—as, he thought with a wry little upward quirk of his mouth, had young Prince Ahmose.

Ah yes, Ahmose. *"Save us from clever princes,"* or *however the quote goes. Wonder what would happen if I challenged him to a race.*

Now for the sword. Some Immortals, he knew, grew almost emotionally attached to their blades. As for him, no. Whatever blade felt right, trustworthy, and properly balanced in his hand was good enough.

As was this one, fine and strong, with no distracting—
and metal-weakening—ornamentation. Letting his face
settle into a tranquil mask, Methos began a series of slash,
guard, thrust, guard, cut left, cut right, lunge—

Right at the face of a servant, the same one who'd
arranged the room for him this past night. The man could
hardly avoid alarm at finding himself suddenly facing a
stark-naked, sword-wielding warrior, but after the first
start, his well-schooled face revealed nothing.

"Does my lord require my services for his morning
grooming?"

*Of course he's calm. In these uneasy times, he has to be
used to the sight of weapons. And of course a guest room
has no lock, and a servant need not knock.*

"Thank you," Methos said urbanely, trying not to pant,
"but no. I really have no need for a servant. Tell your master or masters, if you would, that I shall be out and about
shortly."

The still studiously blank-faced man bowed and left
without a word. It was easy enough to dress in the white
kilt and wide, nicely beaded red and blue necklace that had
been laid out for him last night. Methos slipped his feet
into woven palm frond sandals, wriggling his toes, then, in
the spirit of "one never knew," also buckled his swordbelt
around his waist.

With a fatalistic shrug, he left the room, to find himself,
not surprisingly, with an instant escort of guards. Behind
the guards:

"Ah, Prince Ahmose. The gods send you a good morning."

The young prince dipped his head politely. He looked,
Methos noted, amused, quite weary. *That must have been
quite a report sweet Tiaa delivered!*

"Walk with me a bit," Ahmose said. "Let us enjoy the
morning air."

Methos strolled beside him, aware of the guards keeping
a wary eye on his sword—aware, too, that if he'd been al-

lowed to keep it in the royal presence, he was well on the way to acceptance.

"Thank you for the visit from Tiaa," he said without warning.

Ahmose, for all his princely training, was still too young not to show his surprise. "She told you, then."

"About your orders? She did." Methos glanced sideways. "You aren't going to have her punished for confessing?"

"Of course not! One does not damage a work of art!"

"Or so useful a weapon."

That startled a laugh out of the prince. "Indeed."

Precocious and *clever.*

They walked on for a time, across a garden still wet with dew and heady with the fragrance of the water lilies, the only sound the chirping of sparrows and hum of insects. Methos waited patiently.

Sure enough, Ahmose finally burst out, "Aren't you going to ask me why I sent her?"

"No." Methos waited just long enough after that to see Ahmose frown, then added, "Were I in your place, I don't doubt I'd have been wary of me, too. We do not trust easily, you and I."

"I . . . dare not. And you?"

"I dare not, as well. For, shall we say, somewhat different reasons."

Ahmose could only take that to mean he had some perilous personal enemies. *Close enough to truth,* Methos thought. *The Game hardly allows for many friendships.*

The prince was still frowning slightly, studying him. "You aren't angry."

"At what? At you? For giving Tiaa and me a most delightful evening? Prince Ahmose, I think we understand each other too well for anger."

"Do we?" In the two words was a world of warning: Do not presume.

"Oh, yes," Methos said calmly. "Whatever differences

there may be between us, there is one thing that we have in common: Prince Ahmose, we are both survivors."

That earned him a sharp, cool glance that had nothing of boyishness about it. "Gods grant. Methos, you have recently come down from the Hyksos lands. What can you tell me?"

Methos, who wasn't about to make the mistake of underestimating this youngster, told him frankly, "Not as much as you might like; I removed myself from them as quickly as possible. You already know that the invaders have better weaponry, plus the use of horses."

Ahmose bit back what clearly was going to be an unregal oath. "Yes. I warned my father—the God Sekenenre—I—I warned him we must be better prepared, but he . . . he . . ."

The boy is still very young. Yes, and for all his cleverness, out of his depth.

"Prince Ahmose," Methos said, "your well-being, the well-being of Egypt, is mine, too. And we both know," he added at the prince's wry glance, "that I am not being altruistic about this. Merely honest. We both wish to go right on surviving."

"And you have a plan to help us do just that?"

"An idea," Methos corrected, "or at least the dawning of one."

He waited, testing.

"We shall discuss it," the prince said after only the slightest of pauses. "With, of course, my divine brother."

"Of course." *It took you a moment to remember him, didn't it, Ahmose? But remember him, you did. Ambitious, then, but not fratricidal. Interesting.*

And who knew but that the fact might also be potentially useful?

Survivors, Methos thought.

Chapter Seven

Egypt, Thebes: Reign of Pharaoh Kamose,
1573 B.C.

Kamose, Methos decided several days later, watching
the young pharaoh stalk about the royal courtyard with a
warrior's brusque stride, was not stupid, merely hot-
headed. Like his father.

And, like his father, he seemed given to rhetoric. Never
mind that Methos had a plan to discuss, never mind that it
concerned exactly what both brothers wished most to hear.
No, first the pharaoh must be allowed full vent to his frus-
trations.

*He's not the first ruler I've waited out. And I doubt he'll
be the last.*

To be fair, most of the past few days had been full of
speeches as Kamose had continued to consolidate power
and prove to the people that, yes, they did still have a
pharaoh. It must be difficult for such a young man to shift
out of speech-making fashion, particularly when he was
fighting an uphill battle on an almost daily basis with a
timorous royal court that did *not* want to take on the
Hyksos might.

*But the only people here right now—aside from those
guards lurking back there in the shadows pretending to be
rocks—are your brother and me,* Methos thought. *Relax,
Kamose, relax!*

No. The pharaoh continued to pace, snapping out, "We have been idle too long!"

"What," Ahmose asked warily, "would you have us do?"

"Do? What do you think?" Pace, turn, pace. "We have suffered many insults, brother, far too many, and kept our silence. But now—this—the murder of our father, of a *pharaoh*—no!" He stopped short, glaring. "No matter what those cowards all say, this cannot be tolerated!"

"No," Ahmose said shortly, "it cannot. But—"

"No more excuses! No more ditherings and cowardice! How can I call myself a ruler when there is a king in Avaris, a king in Kush, each man holding a slice of the land, *our* land? How, when I am caught between the Hyksos and the Nubians? No more of this! I shall sweep the Hyksos from Egypt!"

Of course you will, Methos thought wearily. *The Hyksos will run in terror from the sound of your voice.*

With great restraint, he began, "It's all well and good to want revenge, Sire. And, aside from the insult to your country, I don't blame you at all for wanting blood to avenge your father. But," he added with a subtle glance at Ahmose, "the Hyksos have better swords and bows. More to the point, they also have chariots and, above all, horses."

"None of which," Ahmose reminded them darkly, "we are permitted by our kind overlords."

"The Hyksos," Methos said to the air, "are far from here."

"Spies are not."

"Spies," Methos retorted, "are finite, fallible beings, as I am sure you know, Prince Ahmose." He saw the young prince blink at the veiled reference to Tiaa. "They cannot be everywhere at once. Always assuming, of course," Methos added very delicately, "that they are but mortal men."

"Are you claiming to be otherwise?" Ahmose asked, just as delicately.

Methos sat back, watching both brothers through half-lidded eyes. "Do you know that the palace servants have taken to calling me the 'man sent by the gods'?" *Thank you, Queen Teti-sheri, for that.* "What if I really were such a one?"

That made both brothers pause for just a wondering moment. Then Kamose snorted and Ahmose, ah, Ahmose glanced almost admiringly at Methos. Who smiled, ever so slightly and neither claimed or denied anything.

Always keep your hosts off balance. It's so much safer that way!

"Very well, then, 'man sent by the gods,' " Kamose said, "what would you have us do? Merely sit like chastened hounds and do nothing?"

"That is exactly what I propose."

Before Kamose could explode, Ahmose held up a hand. "In other words," he said thoughtfully, "*pretend* to do nothing."

Methos gave him a cursory bow: At least one of the brothers saw where he was heading! "Precisely. Pretend that your spirit is broken. Present a submissive face to the Hyksos. After all, it can't be too long before word of the new pharaoh reaches the ears of the Hyksos king . . ."

"Apophis," Ahmose supplied.

"Yes. Apophis. He will certainly send an envoy to Thebes to find out the truth."

"And collect tribute," Kamose muttered darkly.

"All the more reason not to act prematurely. Because, oh royals, all the while we seem so very humbled, why, we shall be mustering our secret army."

"What army?" Kamose snapped. "Where are we to get the weapons? And, while we're at it, the warriors?"

Methos caught himself about to toss off some easy words about new generations always being born. No, curse it, these were mortals. He, with the easy confidence of an Immortal, might see time as insignificant, but they could not.

Still, it could be done . . . it could, indeed . . . and well within one mortal life span.

"It will not be easy," he began. "And it will not happen

in a day. It will also mean postponing your revenge, oh pharaoh—but," Methos hurried on before Kamose could interrupt, "is not revenge the sweeter when it isn't a man or even a god-king being avenged, but an entire nation?"

Oh, very good, he congratulated himself sardonically. *You should be an orator.*

But the brothers were still listening, so Methos continued, "The Egyptians who I—who my grandfather knew ..." quick save, there, "those Egyptians held a strong love of country. I cannot believe that even a hundred years of occupation has turned them into slaves."

"It has not." Ahmose bit off each word.

"So much for our warriors," Kamose cut in. "Untrained peasants. And for their weapons, what? Clubs? Stones?"

"It seems to me," Methos said to no one in particular, "that, without taking anything away from the god-king's wisdom or knowledge"—a polite nod to Kamose—"there is a vast body of potential knowledge going untouched. Neither of you—your pardons, royals—can pass unnoticed among the common folk. But I can."

"Not alone," Ahmose said shortly. "I will come, too." At his brother's startled glance, the young prince shrugged, "I've done it before." That widened Kamose's eyes even more, but Ahmose said impatiently, "I cannot gain enough experience of how the common people think if I am cooped up in a palace."

"The danger—"

"Oh, brother, what danger? If we cannot trust our own people ..." To Methos he added dryly, "No fear. I shall not be recognized."

No, he would not. Methos, eyeing the young "peasant farmer" at his side a short while later, had to admit that the disguise was excellent.

Until he opens his mouth and spoils the effect with an aristocrat's accent.

But as they went down into the crowded, noisy, dusty Theban marketplace, Ahmose said nothing, only followed

Methos like a mute younger brother down the rows of stalls shaded by awnings of bright colors and many fabrics, followed and watched with intense interest.

Methos squatted down in the shade beside a stocky, middle-aged metalsmith sitting cross-legged behind his low table of wares beating the final shape into a bronze ewer. "Nice work."

The man grunted his thanks.

"Can you do other designs? Custom orders?"

The metalsmith glanced up briefly from his work. "Of course. What smith couldn't?"

"How about this? Could you make something like this? Many copies of it?"

All craftsmen kept piles of broken potsherds and fragments of charcoal handy: convenient and free materials for sketching trial designs. Snatching up one of the potsherds and a bit of charcoal, Methos quickly sketched what was unmistakably a Hyksos sword and showed it to the smith.

"Could you, perhaps, work *this* design?"

The smith glanced up sharply in suspicion. But then he took a good look at his visitor, and sudden recognition flashed in his eyes.

Of course, Methos thought. *Palace gossip flies like the proverbial wind. By now, everyone is going to recognize the stranger who* almost *looks Egyptian.* Not exactly a comfortable thought for someone who generally preferred not to be recognized.

Sure enough, the smith was exclaiming, "The man sent by the gods! Damned right I could. Moving against those bastards, are we? This time doing it, God Sekenenre forgive me, right?"

"I can say nothing."

"Of course not. Me neither. Just give me the right dimensions and weight, yes, and enough bronze, too, and I'll turn out as many swords as the metal will bear!"

"Excellent," Methos said, and got to his feet.

He moved through the marketplace from stall to stall after that, trailed by Ahmose, quietly asking each craftsman or -woman if this or that new design could be worked. And almost each time he received a quick, eager response. A weaver agreed that she could turn out good bowstrings. A maker of furniture nodded with excitement over the thought of bows and chariot wheels. For was the "man sent by the gods" not among them?

"You see?" Methos asked Ahmose after they had circled the marketplace and returned to the palace entrance. "A good deal of enthusiasm there. Granted, this is only the barest of beginnings, but—"

"It could be done, oh 'man sent by the gods,'" Ahmose's face was carefully blank.

Ah. The dark god Envy raises his ugly head. "It's a useful epithet," Methos said flatly. "That doesn't mean either of us need believe it."

"Of course not," just as flatly.

"To continue, Prince Ahmose, you seem to have craftsmen aplenty in Thebes, refugees from Memphis as well as your own citizens. What about the raw materials we'd need?"

"We can get those. The Hyksos expect a steady flow of crafts from us and wouldn't notice a larger supply of wood or bronze if it came in small but constant shipments." Ahmose's eyes blazed in sudden excitement. "We could do this. We really could do this."

"Only if your people work in secret."

"They can, they will! My brother will issue a secret statement, and the literate will read it to those who cannot."

"And your guards will stop anyone leaving Thebes without authorization," Methos added coldly, "and your bowmen shoot down any bird capable of carrying messages. You cannot risk spies, Prince Ahmose."

The glance the prince shot him was just as cold. "There shall be none. So, now: Our craftsmen shall turn their hands to making weapons, and our workers all to learning weaponry. But military training takes space. And if the Hyksos send envoys . . ."

Methos shrugged. "What will they see but normal, everyday life? Keeping your army-in-the-making a secret isn't that great a problem—always assuming, of course, that your people are trustworthy and sufficiently disgusted by Hyksos rule." His gesture took in the vast expanse of desert beyond the city walls. "There's more than enough emptiness out there."

Ahmose laughed. "We could hide an entire army and no one would be the wiser. And yes, our people are trustworthy, and oh yes, but they are weary of Hyksos rule! We can do this. And," he added, voice tight with excitement, "we will. This time we will bring the battle right to Apophis's door!"

Methos held up a warning hand. "All the weapons and warriors in the world aren't going to mean a thing unless you have matching military intelligence. Do you know the layout of Avaris? No? Then you don't know how much force is surrounding King Apophis, either, or how to get at him. Before you can plan any kind of an attack, someone is going to have to get into that Hyksos stronghold."

The boy's face had fallen, for an instant making him look very much only his age. "Yes. . . ." Ahmose agreed pensively, and the boyishness slid away once again. "But . . . a common spy would never be allowed into Avaris. We need someone who would have a very good reason for being admitted—someone who is aristocratic and urbane enough to pass as . . . to pass as an emissary suing for peace."

"Oh now, don't look at me! I'm not even an Egyptian."

Ahmose's smile was predatory. "All the better."

"Because no one will mourn me if I don't come out again? *I'll* mourn me!"

I suppose I should be flattered that the boy trusts me so fully, Methos thought.

Does he?

Should he?

And is this his way of devious revenge on the "man sent by the gods"?

Whatever the motive, the idea was logical enough. Clever and Immortal both, was he not more likely than some poor mortal spy to survive, and to succeed?

Heroes, Methos snapped at himself, *get monuments. Which they usually don't live to see.*

But it wasn't safe to leave the young prince holding the whip hand, as it were. Methos smiled his most carefully enigmatic smile at Prince Ahmose and bowed ever so graciously. "If you wish me to visit King Apophis, honestly wish it, why, who am I to deny a royal request?"

That had exactly the desired effect, clearly making the young prince wonder, *Was he too swift to accept? And why?*

Always keep your hosts off balance, Methos repeated to himself with an inner laugh. *It truly is safer that way.*

More entertaining, as well.

Heroes, Methos kept reminding himself through the following days, as the embryonic Egyptian army made its first tentative moves, *don't live to admire their monuments.*

But he saw more and more examples of how the Hyksos were hurting trade, culture, the very life of Egypt: a farmer begging in the streets of Thebes because his land had been confiscated in King Apophis's name, a woman weeping silently, agonizingly, because her man had been slain by a Hyksos soldier for failing to show proper respect—small matters, small lives, adding into a tragic whole.

These are not my people. This is not my affair.

Yet the idea of worming his way into Avaris and King Apophis's confidence, of doing what no one else could do, was growing so very . . . intriguing.

"I don't want you to go," Tiaa pouted in his ear late one night. Stroking his chest with a warm little hand, she added, "You should stay here. With me. Where you'll be safe."

Methos caught her hand before it could stray any farther south. "With you, my sweet, I am hardly safe. And if I stay here, *Egypt* is not safe."

"Huh? What *does* that mean?"

But he didn't answer her. Staring blankly up into space, Methos realized with a start that, illogical or not, he had come to feel almost proprietary about Egypt.

Now, isn't this ridiculous?

But, more perilously, he was actually angry that Egypt, *his* Egypt, the tranquil, seemingly eternal land that was his occasional sanctuary, should have been so harmed. And was it arrogance to feel that he could restore it? Or was it merely fact?

Of course. They can use that as your epitaph: "He lost his head over Egypt."

"Never mind," Methos told Tiaa. "Now, my dear, where were we . . . ?"

Dowager Queen Teti-sheri had come to the royal court as she did from time to time, presumably, Methos thought, to admire her grandsons—and to be sure they did nothing that was not correctly pharaonic.

But it was he she was watching this morning, her eyes stabbing at him, and Methos dipped his head to her in courtesy.

"Come, approach." Her voice was autocratic. "Away from the rest. We must talk."

"About . . . Avaris?" he hazarded.

"Precisely that." The queen looked up at him. "You have not yet decided what to do."

Either her Gift was very real, or she was an amazing judge of even the slightest hint of expression. "No, I have not. Queen Teti-sheri, I—"

"You must go. You cannot die as other men." Ignoring his involuntary start, the queen continued, "You will be quite safe."

"Your Majesty, believe me, I *can* die, and I would just as soon go right on living!"

She shook her head. "You are the man sent by the gods. They will protect you."

And do the gods know that?

But it was useless to argue with this small, determined, Gifted woman. "Tell me, if you would, Queen Teti-sheri," Methos began, not quite sure if he was being facetious, "has your Gift shown me surviving Avaris?"

A pause. "It does not show you dead."

"Which isn't precisely the same thing." He already knew that the Hyksos were not precisely gentle. And the thought of an Immortal's endless capacity for healing and, with that, the endless capacity for torture . . .

"You will be protected," the queen said stubbornly, and would say nothing more.

But then a flurry of excitement shook the court as a messenger came running, throwing himself down, panting, at Pharaoh Kamose's feet. Kamose, Methos knew, had inherited his father's lookout system, whereby word would be sent from man to man up the Nile to Thebes. And now the message was:

"There is a Hyksos ship on the Nile, great pharaoh, heading toward Thebes! It bears a Hyksos envoy—a tribute collector, oh pharaoh. More, with that one is King Apophis's own half-brother, the royal Prince Khyan!"

Khyan? Methos remembered the street gossip he'd overheard when he had first arrived in Egypt, the discontented murmurings in port. There'd been something about that name . . . *Ah yes, the crazy prince. Not that street gossip about enemy royalty is going to be exactly reliable.*

"So be it," Kamose said regally, and if he was disturbed, not a trace of that showed on his face. He was, Methos thought, learning—on the job, as it were. "We shall," the pharaoh said with only the faintest hint of anger in his voice, "be ready."

Within a few days, the Hyksos envoy arrived, all striped finery and fringes about a stocky form and cold, broad face. With him came a sizable entourage of servants and hard-eyed guards.

But Methos, coming starkly alert, hardly noted any of

them, for the last sensation he would have wanted just now
was suddenly blazing through him, warning:

An Immortal! Here—where?

There.

Beside the envoy stood a tall young man, more slender
than the Hyksos norm, his dark robes glittering with gold.
He was olive-skinned and handsome in a sharp-boned
way—and as he stared at Methos, his dark eyes were fierce
with an eerie fire that could only mean one thing.

Just what I didn't need, Methos thought. *The king's
'half-brother' is both an Immortal and—oh yes, the gossip
was right after all—quite insane!*

Chapter Eight

Egypt, Thebes, and the Nile Valley: Reign of
Pharaoh Kamose, 1573 B.C.

This, Methos thought, staring at Prince Khyan, who
looked as fierce and dangerously fragile as a glass blade,
really wasn't the time or place to meet another Immortal.
It really, truly wasn't.

Particularly not an Immortal with Hyksos sensibilities
and such blatantly shaky mental health.

He dared not wait for Khyan's first move—which was
almost certainly going to be a mindless attack.

When in doubt, bluff.

Forcing his most charming smile onto his face, Methos
stepped forward with open arms (and a readiness to duck
should Khyan lunge). "Why, is this not the famous Prince
Khyan? How wonderful to actually meet you at last!"

All about him, he could hear startled, uneasy murmurings from Egyptians and Hyksos alike, but he ignored
them, concentrating only on his target. The prince drew
back from him as he approached, blinking and confused,
and Methos stopped, continuing in a rush of smooth words,
not wanting to push too hard *or* give the man room to draw
his sword, "But you do not know me. Of course not! How
could you?

"Come, come, will you not walk with me? Leave these
petty matters"—his sweep of an arm took in the Hyksos
envoy and entourage—"to underlings."

Get this weird-eyed prince onto Holy Ground as quickly as possible. And hope he knows what that means.

One of the many royal chapels stood nearby; he wasn't sure which god it honored, but he wasn't going to be picky. *Any* Holy Ground was good enough right now.

He actually did get the prince walking with him, heading toward the chapel—for a few precious steps, at any rate. But then Khyan stopped short, frowning. "Why did I feel . . . that weirdness . . . ?"

"Of course you felt it! You are like me! Yes, yes," Methos rushed on, "we are of the same sort. Isn't that splendid? Now, just a little farther and we can have the privacy to talk—"

"Wait," the prince said firmly. "If you are like me, then that can only mean that you, too, have been singled out by a god—" Khyan broke off abruptly, hand closing about sword hilt. "By an enemy god!"

Damn. "Now, why should you think it an *enemy* deity? Methos purred. "Am I an Egyptian?"

"Yes—"

"No. I am *not* Egyptian, no more than are you! I am not an Egyptian, Prince Khyan, and my gods are not their gods."

That confused Khyan enough to make him slowly let his hand slip from the sword. *Good,* Methos thought, *very good.* He added in a conspiratorial whisper, "Who are they back there? Insignificant little mortals."

Khyan snickered at that, and Methos smiled thinly and continued, "The two of us are so much more than those petty little people. Have we not both been touched by Divine Forces? Neither of us can die! That makes us brothers, Prince Khyan, not enemies!"

The prince straightened. "I already have a brother." That was said, unexpectedly, in a perfectly sane, cold voice. "He is King Apophis, whom all hail."

"Whom all hail," Methos agreed. "A most mighty king, a brave and honorable king—one whom I would dearly love to meet."

And I have just committed myself to it, haven't I? Or at least, he added thoughtfully, *up to a point.*

So now, in for the kill: "Prince Khyan, your coming here is a stroke of the best good fortune for me, for us both. You can get me out of this snare and take me to King Apophis."

"Why?"

"Why!" Why, indeed? "Why, because . . ." Methos continued after the smallest of hesitations, letting his voice drop once more to that conspiratorial whisper, "because I am, as I say, not an Egyptian. I have been caught here, among these lesser beings, for far too long. You understand that, surely!"

"Yes, yes! Continue!"

"I am weary of this place, weary of giving them smooth words—weary of wasting my talents! I could be so useful to King Apophis, so helpful to your brother—and I don't wish to be trapped here, not when there is such power as there is in Avaris!

"In short, I wish to join the winning side, Prince Khyan, the one for whom my powers can do the most good. And . . . oh, but I do admire King Apophis." *Hah.* "What a fine, intelligent, noble man he must be!"

Ah yes, he had gambled correctly. Those had been exactly the right choice of words, because Khyan's eyes blazed with delighted excitement. "It's true!" he exclaimed. "My brother is the finest of men, the truest of brothers—he loves me. Even when I . . . when I am sometimes . . . troubled, when other men might shun me, he—he never shuns me. Not even . . ." the prince's voice shrank to the barest murmur, "not even when he learned the secret."

"That you cannot die?"

"No! No one knows that. Save for you."

Then there could be only one other possibility. Greatly daring, Methos said, in his most mysterious voice, "But there *is* something else . . . I sense it now . . . a dark secret surrounding your birth."

"You can't know that!" It was nearly a shriek. "Only my brother and I know it!"

Gently, now, before he panics. "Ah, but remember that you and I truly are of the same kind! You are not of the royal blood—no shame in that," Methos continued soothingly. "This is nothing more, nothing less, than one of the signs by which one can know he has been 'touched by the gods.' A being with our divine might can never be born of mere mortal man and woman. He must always be found as a babe, raised by those who do not know his power."

That sounds too bizarre for even a madman to believe. And yet ... well ... we all are foundlings.

Khyan, though, seemed perfectly willing to accept the strangeness without question. "You *are* wise. Wise—yes, too wise to be left here among these creatures. You will," he said firmly, "come with me to Avaris."

"You ... never knew there were others like you, did you?" Methos tested. "No one ever told you about ... the Game?"

"What nonsense is this? Games have nothing to do with this!"

Oh, wonderful. No rules.

"You *shall* come with me!" Khyan insisted.

"And there shall be peace between us," Methos intoned solemnly, mental fingers crossed.

"There shall be peace."

But that eerie fire smoldered in the depths of Khyan's eyes. *An uneasy truce at best,* Methos thought. *But at least it is a truce.*

Queen Teti-sheri, you had better be correct. It looks as though I'm about to test your Gift to its fullest extent!

The matter of the tribute was settled, much to Methos's relief, in a day. He didn't think he could have kept the insane prince patiently waiting for his new "brother" for much longer!

That evening, Methos requested and was granted a secret meeting with Kamose and Ahmose. "You may hear

He must not know; he would not comprehend. But you would.

"It was five years ago, five years and three days. We went out hunting into the desert, my brother and I and our warriors, and we killed three lions; *I* killed one, with my arrows.

"But then . . . then as we went riding back to Avaris, a terrible hot wind began to blow, and the sand came before it in a mighty wave. Our horses screamed and ran in terror, and I—I was thrown from my chariot. I tried to call out, but the wind ate my words. I tried to find the others, but the world had gone black with sand and I could not see. I could not breathe! The sand . . . the sand flew into my eyes, my ears, it filled my nostrils and my throat. It stopped the air in my lungs, and I . . ."

Khyan swallowed hard, clearly back in that terrifying time. Methos waited, knowing what as coming.

"I died," the prince said at last. "I died in that desert waste. It was so, this was no dream or false imagining. I died.

"But the great god Set—he to whom the desert waste pays homage—the great god Set brought me back to life. I sat up and brushed the sand from me, and I could breathe and hear and see. The storm was past, and I stood and called till the others found me.

"Set saved me. Set gave me new life. And now I am his son. Now I cannot ever die."

Unspoken in his voice was, *The god who shelters* you *is inferior. The god who shelters you cannot stand before the might of Set!*

Methos was far too wise to argue theology—particularly not with an Immortal who didn't know the Rules of the Game, and who might slide into violence at any time.

As their ship neared the Hyksos capital, Methos watched the massive fortress of Avaris loom up before them. He also saw a new row of stakes with fresh heads upon them, and felt an involuntary shudder shake him.

Khyan laughed. "Afraid?"

"Merely, ah, startled. Those are not the prettiest of ornaments, you must admit."

"But they are! Beheading is the way we execute our traitors!"

"So I gathered."

It didn't help his uneasiness to hear Khyan laugh again and add casually, "Of course they are beheaded. Then disemboweled, so that our sages may read the omens in their entrails. Sometimes," the prince added with a quick flash of his teeth, "this happens *before* the beheading. That is a fascinating sight to watch! We wait and wonder at the sacrifice's stamina, and sometimes we even wager, just a bit, on the length of the screams and how long the life may last."

The worst of it was that he wasn't trying to shock Methos. To Khyan, watching a sacrifice die in utter agony was a pleasant, perfectly normal proceeding.

And here I was beginning to feel sorry for him.

Voice perfectly controlled, Methos said, "Forgive a foreigner his ignorance. But if I may ask, to which gods are these sacrifices made?"

"Why, to our patron god, of course! To *my* patron god! All hail Set, Lord of the Foreign Lands, Bringer of Storms, God of the Desert Waste!"

All hail Set, Methos thought dourly. *Of course they'd worship him!*

Set, whom the Egyptians claimed had murdered his own divine brother, Osiris, for the heavenly throne. Set, who reveled in desert wastes and utter desolation. Set, who was as close to a demon as any god could get.

What better deity could there possibly be for these folks?

Chapter Nine

New York City, Midtown Manhattan: The Present

"Well?" Methos asked over the case holding the Hyksos sword, there in the Branson Collection in New York City. "What else did you expect me to say? Or rather," he added calmly, "what *would* you want me to say? I'm not a mystic, MacLeod, not any kind of a seer, nothing more than an ordinary guy."

And I, MacLeod thought, *am Robert the Bruce.* "Older than most," he murmured, and was rewarded with the barest flicker of amusement on Methos's face. "In fact, I'd say that—"

"There you are!" a sudden voice called. "Enjoying the exhibit?"

"Ah, Professor Maxwell."

As the little man came scurrying forward, at least two books tucked under one arm, together with what looked like quite a bit of paperwork, as well as a much-rumpled newspaper, MacLeod just barely managed to turn his amused grin into a friendly smile. "Yes, I'm enjoying it very much. In fact"—including Methos in the gesture—"we're both enjoying it."

Methos was showing every sign of being about to slip unobtrusively away, but MacLeod, acting on a mischievous whim, caught him by the arm. "Professor Maxwell, I'd like you to meet an old acquaintance of mine."

He watched the two men do the "Albert Maxwell, Adam Pierson" round of courtesies. MacLeod added, still on the same whim, "Adam here is quite knowledgeable about the Hyksos. Almost personally so, in fact."

"*Are* you?" the professor squeaked in delight. "Oh, but then you must join us for lunch, mustn't he, Duncan?"

MacLeod shrugged, held up a hand: Of course! Methos clearly was about to offer some regretful refusal—but then, with a sly sideways glance at MacLeod, said instead, "Professor Maxwell, I would be delighted."

The Branson Collection's little dining room was painted in quietly elegant shades of peach and cream, and tastefully hung with floral prints. But it had once, MacLeod mused ironically, been part of the servants' quarters.

Branson would have been mortified to think of anyone serving lunch to gentlefolk in here, let alone charging them for it. Or maybe, come to think of it, the old robber baron would have been downright amused.

At any rate, the food was agreeable, the service attentive. Methos was being perfectly charming—as, MacLeod thought wryly, he could have predicted—listening intently to Professor Maxwell's theories about the Hyksos and Egyptians without once refuting him, discussing his own "theories" as well, tiptoeing delicately over details that no one other than a firsthand observer (or a New Age fanatic) could have known.

"And so you agree that the Hyksos continued trading with Cyprus," the professor said earnestly, "at least from the evidence at Tell el-Yahudiya; that, of course, is the site near the excavations at Tell e'Dab'a—Avaris, that is—near the Nile Delta."

"Of course," Methos agreed. "Though not all the Cypriot ware came directly from the source. We must not neglect the fact that Malta was a major shipping port—and that the Hyksos were avoiding contact with the Minoans."

"Of course, of course!" Maxwell interjected enthusiastically. "But it's difficult to be sure exactly, without sufficient numbers of artifacts, or much in the way of written records."

"Oh, the Hyksos had a written language. They just weren't so enthusiastic about using it. At least," Methos added with an urbane smile, "so I believe. Admittedly without much concrete proof."

Charming, yes. In fact, MacLeod realized, Methos was being so charming that he, himself, was gently but firmly being shut out of the conversation. For all his knowledge of the art world and its history, he had to admit that the Hyksos weren't really a part of it.

Ye brought it on yerself, me boy, he thought in a deliberate parody of his own once-upon-a-time thick Scottish brogue. *Never try to outclever the clever.*

A polite waiter whispered in Professor Maxwell's ear. "Oh, blast!" the professor exploded, glancing at his watch. "Another meeting, and here I've lost track of the time again. Gentlemen, I *am* sorry to have to eat and run, as it were. I enjoyed our little talk, Mr. Pierson. And please, let's try to do this again, both of you, sometime when things aren't quite so hectic!"

There was the quick, expected fight over the bill: MacLeod won. Professor Maxwell scrambled to his feet, and in the process dropped two books and all of his papers. In his frantic haste, he then got in the way when all three men tried to gather everything back up again, so that MacLeod and Methos banged heads and nearly fell over. The confusion continued until the now thoroughly flustered professor, clutching papers and books to him, finally managed to scurry off.

"Wait," MacLeod called after him, "you forgot your—" but the professor was already out of earshot, and he finished lamely, "newspaper."

He and Methos exchanged a wry grin. "I'd say," Methos commented mildly, "that he was finished with it."

"There's a safe guess. Almost the first thing Professor Maxwell did when we met was point out that grotesque crime story to me. The one," MacLeod added dryly, brandishing the paper at Methos, "that you've been avoiding."

But Methos, to MacLeod's surprise, snatched the paper from him, all humor gone from his face, staring at the front-page photo and the garish WEST SIDE SLAYER KILLS AGAIN headline. "I . . . don't believe it."

"Believe what? What's so alarming?"

Methos shook his head, busily leafing through the paper for the rest of the story. He scanned it, read it again more closely, then glanced up at MacLeod. "Not alarming so much as surprising. You're right; I was avoiding all the charming details of the latest serial killing spree. That's why I didn't know . . ."

"Know *what*?"

Methos was studying the paper again, poring over the front-page photo. "Granted, the media can be overly dramatic. But they didn't invent those beheadings . . . the disembowelings . . . I can't quite make out those signs carved in the earth, or even if those *are* signs; the photos are just too blurry for that. . . . And yet I could almost swear . . ."

"Swear *what*?" MacLeod asked impatiently. "Will you kindly finish a sentence?"

"Ah. Right. I can't be sure, not without a clearer photo, but— Look," Methos interrupted himself, "if we are going to take this discussion any further, I'd suggest we find a more private place."

MacLeod nodded. "The park."

They left the Branson Collection, hurried across Fifth Avenue just ahead of a changing traffic light, and then began to walk up the several blocks' long stretch of unbroken sidewalk on the park side, their voices muffled to any eavesdroppers by the traffic noise.

"As I was saying," Methos continued, "I can't be sure without a much clearer photo. But—I would almost swear that someone is attempting a ritual sacrifice such as the dear old Hyksos used to make."

MacLeod frowned at his calmness. "And no one else

caught the connection? There are enough scholars in a city this size to identify—"

"Ah, not exactly. One of the facts about which I was dancing with your Professor Maxwell is that no one nowadays knows very much about a written Hyksos language: not enough archaeological evidence, I'd guess, because the Hyksos, as I hinted to him, just weren't big on writing things down. The mutilation of the bodies could be just the work of a modern psychopath, while the signs drawn on the earth . . ." He shook his head. "Modern scholars wouldn't be able to identify the symbols as Hyksos."

"Then there's no one but you who knows anything about how the Hyksos used to—" MacLeod broke off, eyeing Methos warily. "I *am* right about that, yes? You *are* the only one? There aren't any Hyksos survivors wandering around, are there?"

Methos opened his mouth, closed it, opened it again. "I don't know," he said at last. "I could have sworn he was dead, though granted I didn't actually take his head." He held up a hand before the impatient MacLeod could interrupt. "Right. I'll get to the point. His name was Khyan, he was one of us—but he was also, at least when I knew him, crazy as the proverbial loon."

"And?"

"And what? Duncan, Khyan could hardly have survived for over three thousand years! He wasn't a bad swordsman—he was bloody good!—but in all that time, insane and frequently unfocused as he was when I knew him, *someone* would surely have taken his head!"

"Would they? These days they call insanity 'mental illness' for a reason. A disease can be cured." MacLeod's mind shied from unwelcome memories of Garrick, hopelessly insane Garrick, who'd nearly driven him insane as well. "Some forms of the disease," he amended. "And," MacLeod continued resolutely, "I'd suspect that was true even in the way-back-when."

"Meaning that Khyan could have survived, sane, for a time? Even, oh, for a millennium or so? Maybe. But sane men don't commit ritual sacrifices in a style three thousand years out of date."

"Maybe," MacLeod said dourly, "he suffered a relapse."

"Very amusing. Look, I can't prove anything one way or the other without something more tangible, such as a clear set of photos. And I doubt that the newspaper personnel are going to grant us those without more of an elaborate charade than I feel like performing right now."

"No need for charades." MacLeod glanced about, getting his bearings. They were midway between Seventy-fifth and Seventy-sixth streets by now . . . yes. "There's a computer rental office not too far away: Third Avenue, somewhere in the eighties. If I can access the paper's Web site, I should be able to get us at least one clear image."

Methos, who, MacLeod suspected, was every bit as technically adept, if not even more, than he, shrugged. "I bow before your hacker expertise. Lead on."

"There," MacLeod said some time later, taking the pages he'd downloaded from the printer. "That's about as clear as the image is going to get."

Methos took the proferred printouts, frowning at them.

"Well?" MacLeod prodded after a while.

A shrug. "I'm not sure. It's been a long time since I've seen any of the Hyksos writing . . . a very long time since I had to actually read any of it. . . ."

Another period of silence.

"Wait, now. . . ." Methos said suddenly. "That could be a god-name . . . and that . . . ha, yes, it's beginning to come back to me." He raised an eyebrow at MacLeod. "It's Hyksos, all right. Nothing coherent, which is what gave me the difficulty, just bits of what looks like a prayer to, I'd guess, the Egyptian god Set. The nasty fellow who murdered his brother god, Osiris."

"I know the story."

"Yes, well, the Hyksos were big on him."

"Nice people."

"Told you."

They left the computer offices, returning to the safer anonymity of the noisy city streets before continuing the conversation.

"Then," MacLeod began, "the West Side Slayer *is* Khyan."

Methos's face was unreadable. "It does seem the most likely possibility. As to why he's here . . . the sword. Khyan can only be hunting the Hyksos sword."

"The one you said held a—a royal soul?"

"He'd believe that. If he's still half as crazy as I think, he would certainly believe that—"

"Then why is he hunting it in Riverside Park? That's the wrong side of Manhattan!"

"—*but*, we will assume, isn't sane enough to find the sword easily. Yes . . . that would be why he's performing those sacrifices: They're appeals to the gods. Khyan knows that the sword is here, he wants it, and he's trying to get the gods, Set in particular, to help him locate it."

"And we," MacLeod said, "have to stop him."

Methos looked at him with absolutely no expression. " 'We.' "

"Come on, Methos! You're the one who knows what he looks like! You want me to call the police and tell them, 'There's a three-thousand-year-old madman sacrificing people, and you can only kill him by cutting off his head'? You know about the Hyksos—and about this Khyan."

"Sorry. I gave up my Boy Scout badges a long time ago."

"Methos."

"And no, I am not going to feel guilty over the antics of a lunatic I didn't get to behead over three thousand years ago."

With great restraint, MacLeod said, "I'm not asking you to be a Boy Scout. But we are faced with an insane Immortal. One who is killing people so that he can perform divinations over their mangled bodies—"

"Exactly. I am, as the saying goes, out of here."

"No, you are not. Think about it, Methos: Even if the po-

lice do manage to track Khyan down and capture him, he's
not going to stay caught for long. Nor is he going to keep
his mouth shut about himself or the rest of us. And a mur-
derous, crazy Immortal who isn't going to worry about
mortals discovering who and what he is—"

Methos held up both hands in resignation. "Is a danger
to all Immortals," he finished. "Yes, right, true enough.
Particularly if he happens to miraculously come back to
life in front of everyone, or is subjected to any in-depth
medical tests. And yes, true enough, I'm the only one who
knows enough about him and his native time and place to
have any hope of stopping him."

"Well?"

"Well, what? I don't have much of a choice, do I? But—
d'you know something, Duncan?"

"What?"

"I really do hate it when you're right."

Chapter Ten

New York City, West Side:
The Present

He woke with a start, for a terrifying time not sure where he was or why the room should seem so . . . wrong. There should be a good, hard bed, a sensible wooden headrest, not this sagging, too-thin mattress. There should be a window set high in the wall to let in the clean desert breeze, not this—this staleness, this ugly, dirty glass through which one could barely see, and see only walls at that, and yet more walls—

Walls, yes, glass, yes.

Realization shook him. This was not the once-and-no-more. This was what these people called the twentieth century. He was still in the city they called New York, still in Manhattan, in the cheap little room he had rented, must have rented (he could not remember how or when), somewhere on the western edge of the island.

Ah. More memory. He had returned here sometime just before dawn, that much he did recall, yes . . . after the sacrifice.

The sacrifice that had failed.

With a shudder, he leaped to his feet, his reflexes still those of the warrior. He was, he noted without surprise, still fully clad, and a sudden surge of caution made him quickly check himself and his sword blade for telltale signs, bloodstains—

No. Nothing to betray him.

There was suddenly a dim memory of other times, other places. He stood stock-still, letting it come as it would, if it would. . . . There had been a—what?—occupation, a series of occupations, times over a long, long span when he was something these people called "sane" (meaningless term, useless term), living in their dull little plane of existence, cut off from the gods, from his god, even a recent space wherein he'd known the means of earning the coins this time and place required.

But now . . . but now . . .

Nothing. Nothing!

Set, he prayed, *Set. Let me not be barred from you. Let me not become not-me.*

He could not hold fast to memories of what he'd done, how he'd lived, and they drifted away. No matter, no matter, he was above small things such as salaries, the worries of commoners.

He wandered from the room, from the house made up of several of these cheap rooms, ignoring the sneers of the rough-faced man behind the front counter—something about "rent," and "stupid Arab," and "come back with it or don't come back."

Words. They meant nothing.

He wandered on, through streets busy with trucks—an area of busy commerce, some fragment of logic told him, not surprising with the river's docks so near. He wandered, drawn to that river. Not the right one, he dimly knew it, not the regal Nile, but sacred, surely, just the same, so broad and with such mighty tides. Staring at it, he knew it was so. The river was sacred, yes, the Great River, this Hudson, and he softly repeated the proper prayers.

Then why would the god not hear? Why would Set not aid him?

But—how could he? Set was, after all, a god of the desert waste. The realization made him shudder: There was no desert here. Did that mean—

No! He could not fail, he would not fail! His brother was

here, somewhere in this city, he knew that, felt that, like a faint voice calling to him, *Here, find me, here. . . .* The voice had brought him to New York—but with all these many lives, how could he ever find . . .

He would not doubt. He would find his brother, help him, even if it meant slaying hundreds for the god, thousands! He would help his brother, though he turned this city into . . .

Was that it? Was that what the god wished?

The force of this new revelation shook him so fiercely that he sank to his knees. Yes, this was the answer, this was the answer!

"Hear me, oh great Set," he cried. "Help me now, and I shall turn this vast city into a desert waste in your holy name."

He spoke in the ancient tongue, dimly aware of passersby, of sneers of "foreigner," meaningless "Arab, betcha." But no one touched him, so he need not heed them. And as he continued his prayers, the watchers drifted away.

"Help me, oh great Set, and I shall slay them all, one by one, ten by ten, a hundred by a hundred. They cannot stop me, they do not know me, they cannot know me.

"For you, oh great Set, have placed your hand upon me and your breath of Life in my nostrils. You have made me your child.

"And I, oh great Set, am truly your son."

And yet, a surge of memory warned him, there was one who might try to stop him, yes . . . one other who had been touched by a god. . . .

The name surfaced without warning: Methos.

Yes, yes, he had not seen that one since . . . since . . . But his mind refused to remember that terrible day, told him only: *That one is here. Methos is here.* For had he not from time to time in this vast city been brushed by that familiar aura, the eerie sureness that he'd been near one touched by a god? Once he'd actually drawn sword and tried to pursue, only to have lost the trace amid the teeming, godless others, then, most shamefully, having been pursued himself by their officers of the law. (And had there not been other times, others he'd fought, yes, and . . . and felt the splendor of the gods enfold him . . . something . . . a Game . . . ? He could not quite remember.)

But it could only be that one. Methos.

Methos, who would try to stop him. Try and fail.

Methos, who would die.

Chapter Eleven

=====

Egypt, Avaris: Reign of King Apophis, 1573 B.C.

"There," Khyan said proudly as the Hyksos ship came broadside to the dock.

As sailors busily raised oars, moored the ship, and lowered the wooden gangplank, Methos stared up at the massive wall surrounding Avaris. The wall, he mused, that looked even more impressive seen up close, particularly since now he could see that it stood on a rampart of earth and stone.

But: *There?* he wondered, looking at the unornamented expanse. *There* where? "Ah?"

"That gate!" Khyan's quick, contemptuous glance said, *Only a fool wouldn't have instantly known what I'd meant!* "That is the only gate by which one may enter Avaris. No enemy may ever invade!"

"Ah." *Never, my mad prince, say "never."*

Still, Methos added to himself as they came ashore, no attack was likely to make it across this exposed field and through that heavily reinforced gate. And it did, indeed, seem to be the only access through the all-too-solid wall.

As Prince Khyan, not waiting for his attendants, strode boldly through, guards barely got the thick, bronze-plated door open in time. The prince kept going, not deigning to notice their salutes or the frantically following retainers, and Methos, perforce, kept going with him, surreptitiously noting every detail of his surroundings as he went. Thick wall, all right, just about . . . hmm . . . one and a half bow-shots thick. No one was going to cut through all that mud brick. And the regularly spaced watchtowers meant no one was going to scale the wall, either.

So then. No possible safe attack from the Nile. Not a frontal attack, at any rate. But what if one came in from the side? Or, for that matter, *under* the wall? No, not likely; an attacker would be pinned down by arrows from above before he could—

"There!" Khyan repeated, and Methos started almost guiltily. The prince was pointing. "There ahead of us is Avaris's heart, the royal citadel itself."

"Ah!" Methos said yet again. *Good, safe, all-purpose exclamation.*

All around them lay a crowded tangle of buildings, without so much as an alleyway separating most of them: The Hyksos citizens attached to the royal court had to live somewhere, and apparently this lot didn't want to try their luck out there with the not necessarily cowed Egyptians—even though space within the walls was clearly at a premium.

Useful fact. Easy to spread plague or fire in here. Always assuming, of course, that one could somehow bypass that cursed outer wall.

Beyond was a second, inner wall, not quite as impressive, the bronze gate of which was flung open at Khyan's autocratic approach. Beyond that lay, surprisingly, some rather handsome gardens, quite beautifully landscaped. But their green loveliness only made the brooding fortress they surrounded look the more menacing by comparison: more thick walls, more square-sided towers. The fortress was basically one great, unornamented rectangle taller even than the outer walls.

Methos fought down the urge to say, *Ugly, isn't it?* "Impressive," he safely chose instead.

Which was, after all, just as accurate.

No answer from Khyan. For want of any other choice,

Methos followed him on into the citadel, down corridors painted with murals it was too dark to see clearly.

They look like Canaanite designs. I think. Well, rumor does have it that the Hyksos are at least first cousins to the Canaanites.

The corridor ended in a sudden blaze of torchlight. Blinking, Methos found himself in the royal audience hall, a large room, shadowy despite the number of torches and smoky because of them. The roof was half lost in darkness, but Methos guessed from what he could make out that it might be made of expensive cedar-wood planking, probably imported from Tyre, its weight supported by sturdy stone columns.

The torches illuminated the predictable crowd of courtiers to be found at any royal court, this lot almost all in the striped, fringed robes that seemed to be in current fashion for the Hyksos.

As Prince Khyan continued his forward march, Methos, following in his wake, had only a brief glimpse of walls painted with more murals, these of lesser deities worshiping a greater—Set, yes, that's who it was, labeled by a cartouche over his head, and dressed up as a Canaanite!—before he was brought up short by guards with crossed spears.

There ahead of him, on a stone chair of a throne, sat the man who, glittering with gold at throat and waist and hilt of sword and dagger, must surely be King Apophis.

The ruler of the Hyksos was of middle years, just at the point when a well-muscled mortal man began to turn to fat. His face was olive-skinned, with wide cheekbones, a jaw that looked strong enough to chew stone, and dark eyes that said their owner had seen a great deal and had given mercy to none of what he'd seen.

Save for the dark hair, now streaked with gray, he looked not in the slightest like Khyan.

So that was why the convenient fiction about Khyan being only a half-brother! *"He doesn't look at all like you,*

King Apophis!" "Really? Congratulations on becoming tonight's sacrifice!" Much safer this way for everyone.

Khyan, impatient with any ceremony, pushed the guards' spears brusquely aside, hurrying straight to the royal throne. "Brother!"

Apophis, to Methos's great astonishment, got to his feet to pull Khyan into a firm embrace. And those cruel, jaded eyes softened for a moment to something approximating genuine love.

So-o! Methos quickly put together what facts were known, extrapolating others: Khyan had spoken often of his brother, rarely of his brother's wives, never of any nieces or nephews. Was that it? If King Apophis had no sons to his name, he might well have poured all his hopes, his frustrated parental longings, on Khyan.

Only to learn too late that said brother is insane. My, my, see what love gets you? A blind spot where the loved one is concerned; a refusal to see the truth.

That he himself had occasionally possessed such a blind spot over the centuries . . . ah, well, no man, not even an Immortal, was perfect.

Ah, but I don't like being on display like a conquered prize. I wonder if there's any way I can just . . . merge with the crowd.

But Apophis had released Khyan, and the cold stare was studying Methos, who, politic behavior being the better part of valor, gave up any attempts to slip away and bowed.

Apophis glanced at Khyan. "Who have you brought me, brother?"

"This . . . this is a valuable ally!" Khyan crowed.

The cold stare never wavered. "And have you a name, oh valuable ally?"

"I am Methos, King Apophis. And I have come—"

A gasp from the crowd cut into his words. The king straightened in his chair, sharp gaze hunting out the one who had dared interrupt, and Methos thought that he'd seen snakes with warmer eyes.

"You." The royal hand stabbed out, and a man flinched. "Step forward."

The man not only stepped forward, he prostrated himself. "Oh mighty king, I meant no disrespect."

His voice was muffled against the stone of the floor, and the king snapped, "Up!"

Scrambling hastily to his knees, the man repeated, "I meant no disrespect. But I know this one—and he is no friend to the Hyksos!"

Damn it to the desert wastes, that's the customs officer. Of all the foul luck—

But luck, Methos had learned over the centuries, was very much what one made it. He would much rather not have had so much hostile attention so suddenly drawn to him, but one took advantage of what was given.

"Do you know me?" Methos purred at the official after only the smallest of pauses, ignoring the startled glance from the king at this arrogance. "Truly know me? Who am I, then?"

"Stand," King Apophis ordered shortly. "Speak."

The customs official shot Methos one quick, nervous glance. "This man, this foreigner, oh king, is someone of no known nation, no known abode. And more, oh king, he—he claims to be a magician!"

A superstitious murmuring raced through the court. Methos, gambling, let out a cold, sharp bark of a laugh, and the murmurings stopped as though cut off by a blade. Into the sudden tense silence he said disdainfully, "Your Majesty, I made no such claim! I spoke the truth, told this . . . underling that I was merely a traveler, a pilgrim of sorts. And if he took those simple words to mean anything else . . ." He shrugged.

"And *are* you a magician?" King Apophis asked.

No verbal clue as to how he should answer. No hint of how the Hyksos felt about magic. Khyan was staring at him as though expecting him to say something wondrous, so Methos, feeling his way, said, "Maybe."

"Maybe!"

"Your Majesty, if I were a magician, what good would boasts do me? And if I were *not* a magician, what good would boasts do me?"

To his relief, King Apophis chuckled at that, and there didn't seem to be active malice in the tone. Khyan laughed, mouth wide like that of a child, and said, "You see, you see? He is an ally, and"—his voice dropped to a fierce whisper—"he has been of—of great help to me. The dreams . . . he has been of great help."

"Has he? I thank you for that," the king said to Methos, and seemed to mean it. "But why are you here?"

"I come in the name of Pharaoh Kamose, oh king, to offer you tribute as is your due."

"Smooth words. And the tribute has, of course, already been accepted. But why are *you* here? You are not, I think, Egyptian."

Shrewd observer: dangerous. "No, Your Majesty, I am not." Methos glanced about. "Your pardon, King Apophis, but is this really for . . . all to hear?"

"No!" Khyan snapped. "No! Brother, we must talk in private!"

Apophis might have been about to say something else, but Methos saw him pause and glance at Khyan, once again with almost gentle eyes, the eyes, Methos thought, of someone used to making allowances for this one soul in all the world.

"So be it," the king said. "All of you: Out."

It took some time before the hall was empty of all but the requisite—and presumably incorruptible—guards. Methos waited with his face fixed in a mask of utter calm, wishing for either a chair or a cool drink. Not likely to get either. Not yet.

"Now," King Apophis said. "Speak, and speak honestly. Who are you and why are you here?"

"Your Majesty, I have already told you my name: Methos. And it is true, I am no Egyptian. Equally true that I came to this land out of no darker motive than curiosity."

"Came? From where?"

"Most recently Albion, King Apophis."

Blankness.

So now, a narrow worldview: Canaan, Egypt, not much more. A useful fact? "That is a cold, damp land," Methos hurried on with a dismissive wave of a hand; one did not point out royal shortcomings to a king. "And so I set sail for a warmer place."

"Sailed where? Where did you stop, Methos?" Khyan cut in. "Before you reached Egypt. Crete? Did you visit Crete?"

His brother gave him a sharp, warning glance, but added, "Well? *Did* you visit Crete?"

His tone was just too casual to be credible. *Crete,* Methos thought, wondering. A quick flash of memory: the mother of Kamose and Ahmose . . . the royal widow whom he'd not yet met since she'd been off in the south, keeping a military watch on the Nubians . . . her name was Ahhotep, and she was partly of—yes, of Minoan blood, from the Cretan royal line!

Very useful! But not to be brought to bear just yet.

"No, King Apophis," Methos said truthfully, "I did not. The ship's master, the captain of the Levantine vessel *Western Bird,* will confirm that fact, if you wish: Albion, Malta, Egypt.

"As for why I am here: I appreciate power, and I appreciate efficiency. Neither of which I found in Thebes."

The king snorted. "In other words, you wish to change sides. Why should I trust someone who has already betrayed his allies?"

"Not my allies," Methos said darkly. "Never my allies. King Apophis, I found myself in Thebes through mere mischance, and had to bide my time till I could also find a safe way out again. And now I am, indeed, out of there, and quite willing to bargain for a more . . . useful position here at a true king's court."

"Bargain."

"Concerning matters Egyptian and . . ." he paused just long enough to make the king tense slightly, then finished,

"Minoan." *Oh yes, that struck a nerve! Uneasy about Crete, aren't we? And I think I can guess why. However . . .* "Ah," Methos added with beautifully feigned regret, "but a king's schedule is always so very full! Surely I cannot take up too much of your time now."

"Never fear. We *will* talk, later."

Did I hear hot irons in your voice? But Methos said cheerfully, "Excellent. I have a great deal of information that I'm certain you'll find useful."

"Oh, I'm certain that you do," the king agreed. "And I do plan to hear it all."

He laughed as though making a pleasantry, but there wasn't the slightest trace of humor in his voice. But Methos's experiences had included a good many encounters with rulers; he'd been expecting some attempt at royal intimidation just about now. Prepared, he merely smiled, in a way he had practiced over the centuries. A world of dark mystery and even darker cruelty was in that smile.

And Methos saw from Apophis's slightest of starts that it was the king who had just been disconcerted.

He really does wonder if I wield magic. Easy now, though. Push a snake too hard, and it strikes.

He quickly let the cold smile warm into a more harmless one, and saw Apophis relax. "So be it," the king snapped. "Brother, see that your guest is given food and lodging."

"Your" guest, is it? Not "our"? Here on royal sufferance, am I?

Good enough. Safe enough.

For now.

Chapter Twelve

Egypt, Avaris: Reign of King Apophis, 1573 B.C.

As he obediently followed Khyan out of the audience hall, Methos released a silent, wary sigh. Gods, he could really use a drink right now, maybe some of that decent beer the Egyptians brewed. Yes, and some nice, friendly, and above all *harmless* drinking companions wouldn't be such a bad idea, either! Such dangerous games as the one he'd just been playing with King Apophis could be entertaining, but they were *not* easy.

And the games are going to continue later today or tomorrow, whenever Apophis decides he's made me wait long enough. Soften up the mysterious stranger a bit.

I don't weaken quite so easily.

But . . . oh, I would welcome that beer, yes, and a peaceful inn around it!

Khyan, not noticing his "guest's" sudden pensiveness, led Methos down a new corridor, then out into a central courtyard bright with sunlight in clear imitation of the Egyptian style. Unlike the Egyptians, though, the Hyksos apparently didn't waste time on any pretty little ponds full of fragrant water lilies—which wasn't to say that the courtyard wasn't . . . ornamented. Methos paused in spite of himself at the realization that the "fruit" one tree bore was actually a neatly arranged hanging display of skulls.

How charming. But then, I used to know some Eastern

tribesmen a few centuries back who drank from their enemies' skulls.

Come to think of it, I didn't care for those folks, either.

"There," Khyan said suddenly.

Now what? "There, Prince Khyan?"

"Do you see that bloodstain?"

No. "Your Highness?"

"That is where I slew a demon, I myself. They said afterward that it was only a steward, but I knew better; demons can transform themselves into any likeness."

"Of . . . course."

"I knew that you would understand! There!"

Methos bit back what would have been a suicidal sigh of impatience. "There?"

"That is the doorway to where you shall lodge."

Let it not be a storage shed, you royal lunatic, or, for that matter, a prison cell.

But it was nothing more or less than a room, clean enough, with a bed in the Egyptian style.

No Tiaa, though, more's the pity. A little softness wouldn't be amiss in this place.

Guards in plenty, though, patrolling ostentatiously about just outside. Well, that was hardly surprising; he wasn't exactly a trusted visitor. Yet.

Or maybe ever.

They did feed him, eventually, and give him something to drink as well, there was that: decent fish and freshly baked bread and, yes, a credible flagon of beer. And there was plenty of oil for the room's one lamp. No one bolted the door on him, either.

But Methos slept very little and very lightly that night. At last, toward dawn, he gave up slumber altogether and lay staring thoughtfully into space. What if . . .

Swinging his feet over the side of the bed, he drew out the amulet of Pharaoh Merneferre Ay.

A shame to damage it after all these years. But better it than me!

Methos, like a good many other travelers crossing and

recrossing the Mediterranean, had picked up a few phrases of the Minoan language, even of the written language, the court language.

A pity I don't have a better tool for this, but . . .

Drawing his sword, he used its point to incise certain Minoan characters onto the back of the amulet, working them into the soft gold with delicate care, swearing a bit under his breath . . .

There. He sat back to study his handiwork, deciding, after a moment, *Good enough.*

Very good, in fact. One might even say, downright seditious.

All there was to do now was wait.

The morning brought not the immediate resumption of hostilities in the form of questioning that he had expected, but, unexpectedly, an invitation to worship. King Apophis, Methos learned from a servant, made offerings to Set in the royal chapel every day.

"Invitation," of course, Methos thought, yawning over the Hyksos equivalent of breakfast—reasonably fresh bread and weak beer—meant, "Attend or regret it!" A blatantly transparent test, naturally, since no Egyptian would dare openly worship so perilous a deity.

I am not an Egyptian, Methos thought, *these are not my gods, and I have more immediate problems than whether or not a deity of the desert waste actually exists and would bother to be interested in me.*

Which didn't mean that he wasn't subject to a purely superstitious thrill of worry as he entered the chapel. But nothing eerie happened—*Of course nothing eerie happened!* Methos chided himself—and the ceremony consisted of nothing more alarming than some rote chanting, in which Methos prudently took part, and an offering, of all unlikely things for a desert deity, of garlands.

One hurdle safely jumped, he thought, eyeing the king eyeing him, and bowed.

Apophis almost smiled. "And now, my brother's friend, we shall continue our conversation."

"Of course we shall," Methos retorted as though delighted. *Always keep your hosts off balance.* "Where would you like to begin?"

Later—much later—Methos stood alone with King Apophis in a private chamber (though, of course, guards lurked just outside). Or rather, he stood, alone, while Apophis sat. Feet and throat weary, and doing his best to hide his uneasiness about being unarmed while another Immortal was somewhere in the area, Methos kept determinedly to his act of "I am absolutely charming," even if the king, by now, was not.

". . . and so, in summation," he continued, not quite watching Apophis, "the new pharaoh is a hot-tempered young man with little military skill." *Save for what he learned in the field, but that, oh King, you need not know.* "His brother is barely out of boyhood and poses no immediate threat." *Save for his cleverness and calculating mind, but again, you need not know that.* "There seems to be little rivalry between the brothers, nothing on which to build, but of course I, as an outsider, could hardly be an accurate judge of that."

"Of course," Apophis echoed dryly. "And their army?"

Methos gave a contemptuous little laugh. "And what army would that be, oh king? When I left them, they had a cavalry consisting of exactly four chariots, all Hyksos-issue, the adequate but not remarkable bronze weaponry I am sure your spies have already described to you, and bows that have perhaps half the range of your own. Again, as you doubtless already know." *All true, all items in the process of being altered—which, I sincerely hope, you do not already know.*

Apophis grunted noncommittally.

"In brief, oh king," Methos continued, "they have no more standing army than ever." *Yet.* "Pharaoh Kamose, if it came to it, might be able to mount a hundred men able to wield weapons with any professional skill, no more than that." *Again, yet.*

King Apophis leaned forward in his chair, eyes predatory. "These are all pretty details, Methos, but surface ones only. Any spy, as you say, could have told me as much. Give me something more. Something I can use. Something," he added, not quite in warning, "that says to me, 'This man is useful, this man is telling me the truth.'"

Methos smiled ever so slightly. "King Apophis, if I tell you all that I know, what's left to keep you from killing me?"

"Clever," the king acknowledged. "I warn you, I am not very fond of clever men."

"Ah, but a clever man knows where he stands. It is far safer, King Apophis, to be beside the throne than on it."

"So now!" the king exclaimed, eyebrows raised. "Do you think so high?"

"Not as high as the throne, I repeat. As you say, I am far too clever to want that burden."

"But you do think to be my advisor?"

"Not without giving you good reason to see my worth."

"Go on. You still amuse me. Don't worry," the king added, "you'll know when you do not."

Methos ignored that. "Oh king, I ask you this: Who is the mother of Pharaoh Kamose and his brother prince?"

"What nonsense is this?"

"Who is their mother?" *Do you really not know or remember? Or are you testing me again?* "Her name is Ahhotep, as of course you know, oh king."

"Of course."

"And Ahhotep, as is no secret, is of two lineages: Egyptian *and* Minoan."

Apophis tensed. "What are you saying? They could *not* have formed an alliance! Kamose could never have sent a message as far as Crete!"

"No?" Methos asked. "Ah, of course not. The Hyksos are mighty warriors, well able to stop the fish in the Nile or the bird in the sky. Particularly," he added lightly, "the bird in the sky."

"But the Egyptians have no carrier birds!"

"No, of course not. King Apophis says it, so it must be so."

"Guard your tongue!"

Methos met Apophis's glare without blinking. "Ah, but the king did command the truth from me. And would I dare to lie, now, with my life at stake?"

For what seemed an unbearably long time, he held the king's stare, projecting with all his will nothing but utter sincerity.

"No," the king muttered at last. "No, you would not. But proof—"

"Your pardon, King Apophis, but I have proof."

Fighting down the urge to reveal it with a magician's flourish, Methos showed the king the amulet of Merneferre Ay—the amulet with that telltale, if false, Minoan inscription. As he'd expected, Apophis couldn't read it, but the king certainly did recognize that, one, the amulet was genuinely royal Egyptian, and two, the inscription was genuinely Minoan.

He glanced sharply up at Methos. "Where did you get this?"

"From the Egyptian royal court," Methos answered, quite truthfully. That it had been a now-long-vanished Egyptian court was immaterial. "The inscription was never meant for my eyes, of course."

"And do you know what it says?"

"King Apophis, as I mentioned, if I tell you all I know—"

"I will not kill you," the king said impatiently. "Not as long as you remain useful. Now tell me what it says."

Methos read, slowly as though being careful to get the words right, " 'It shall be done, our lands united, the foe crushed between us.' "

Apophis said nothing to him, but called for a scholar,

who read the inscription and told his king, "That is, indeed, what is written here."

"Interesting," Apophis said shortly, and meant a great deal more than that. "No," the king added to Methos, "I shall not kill you. You may yet prove very useful, indeed."

Methos bowed, hiding a faint, triumphant smile. *So, King Apophis, may you!*

But he had not lived this long by being careless or, for that matter, cocky. Yes, he had won this particular fight, but it was merely the opening sortie.

He knew perfectly well that the rest of the war remained.

Chapter Thirteen

Egypt, Avaris: Reign of King Apophis, 1573 B.C.

Methos had entered the audience chamber escorted by guards, and he left it escorted by guards, back into the dazzling brightness of the central courtyard.

But the soldiers suddenly drew back—as did Methos a second later, as he found himself facing without warning both the urgent alert of another Immortal's presence and said Immortal's sword point.

"Prince Khyan!"

For a wild instant, he saw himself already dead, stabbed through by the madman before he could move, and his head removed. But Khyan backed off with a laugh, saluting him with the sword.

"Come!" the prince cried. "Come and duel with me!"

I really don't want to duel with you, thank you very much, not with someone who might forget in a moment that we're only playing.

And so Methos smiled and gestured to himself. "As you see, I am unarmed."

"You, or you, give him a sword! Yes, or let him go and retrieve his own!"

"Ah no, Prince Khyan," Methos interjected apologetically. "It isn't that I don't want to duel with you." *Hah.* "But you are a prince, trained as a prince, and I—I am no one! You are surely so fine a swordsman that your very skill would make me far too envious to continue."

Any more sweetness and I may be ill.

But Khyan seemed to accept it all at face value. With a solemn nod, he turned to one of the guards. "You then! Come!"

The guard, having no choice about it, grimly followed Khyan out into the center of the courtyard. Under the tree with the skulls, Methos noted. Fitting.

As Khyan closed with the guard, Methos, slyly watching to be sure the other guards were growing engrossed in the duel, slipped subtly toward his room until he had reached it and could snatch up his sword and belt it about his waist. Just in case.

Feeling a little less naked, he stood in the doorway, watching the duel, lips pursed in a silent whistle. Madman or not, Khyan was a fine swordsman, downright alarmingly fine, quick on his feet and lightning fast with his reflexes. The guard, handicapped by trying not to harm the prince, was at a definite disadvantage.

And then, quite suddenly, he was dead. Khyan, eyes savage, brought his sword sweeping across in a powerful slash that sent the guard's head flying off. It rolled almost to where Methos stood, its eyes and mouth wide as though in utter astonishment that such a silly thing could happen.

As the body fell, spouting blood, Khyan whirled and whirled again, saying to them all, but mostly to Methos, "You saw? You saw? He tried to kill me! I had to defend myself!"

The guards were surely going to protest, or at least show their horror—

But no, they showed not even the politic acceptance Methos might have expected. They were . . . joking. Jesting about their late comrade's poor skills and how he would at least make a decent offering to Set. Survival instincts? Possibly. They had to be grateful they weren't the ones lying dead. But there was a certain indifference to their eyes and voices . . .

Wonderful morale we have here.

But he couldn't concentrate on the potential uses of that

right now, not with Khyan pointing that bloody sword at him.

"It needs cleaning," Methos said so calmly that he surprised himself. "A good blade should not be treated so casually."

And, equally surprising, Khyan looked at the blade, then lowered it. "True." There was no longer the slightest trace of madness in his voice, and his expression looked merely weary. "Quite true."

Does he even remember he just killed a man?

Khyan was busy cleaning the blade free of blood on the edge of his tunic. "You, and you, get rid of that garbage." The wave of his hand took in head and body both. "And clean up the mess."

"My prince . . . ?" One guard began warily.

"No. I—I am tired now. I will rest."

He sheathed his sword with practiced ease, not even needing to glance at the scabbard, then wandered off.

Ah, yes. Welcome to Avaris, Methos told himself. *A whole world of charm.*

The day passed in absolute, unnerving tranquility after that, with nothing more granted to him than a very brief tour around the palace—or what little of the palace he was permitted to see—by a polite but bored servant. Methos dutifully examined murals and carvings, most of which were, as he'd suspected, an uneasy if not unattractive mixture of Canaanite and Egyptian designs, oohed with proper respect at the chapel to Set, with its very realistic paintings of the god beheading his divine brother, and all the while looked for weaknesses in structural design and very gently tried prying what information he could from his guide.

Unfortunately, said guide was wise in the ways of survival, saying only what one would expect from a wary servant: King Apophis was a mighty man, a god among kings, and his half-brother was clearly sacred, touched by the gods. And from what Methos could see from this brief tour, the palace was utterly solid, utterly impregnable.

Frustrating.

Of course, this lack of anything fruitful was deliberate on King Apophis's part: Keep the "guest" in boring comfort until he either betrays himself or proves himself worthy of trust.

Or until Khyan decides to attack me.

At least Apophis hadn't decided to simply put the "guest" to the question, or whatever other idiom they used in this court for king-sanctioned torture. That didn't mean, Methos knew, that he wasn't constantly being watched and judged. The most blatant of the watchers—that is, the one who was trying the hardest not to be seen—was a slender young male servant with the fierce eyes of a born idealist.

Definitely not spying on King Apophis's orders.

A would-be assassin? Or merely a would-be rebel looking for an ally? Either way, Methos thought, an amateur.

King Apophis's spies, by contrast, were so far from amateur that only logic and years of wariness told Methos that they were there at all.

At least I'm establishing myself as harmless. Which is, unfortunately, not exactly the opinion I need to develop.

That night, he spent more time awake and plotting than he did asleep. But no sooner had Methos finally given up on plots and drifted into fitful sleep than he was roughly awakened by the twin alarms of *Immortal, here!* and a terrified scream. He was on his feet in an instant, heart racing and sword drawn—

But Khyan wasn't attacking him. Khyan was standing there in the doorway, blank-faced, shaking and wet with perspiration but clearly not yet truly awake.

"Prince Khyan? Prince Khyan!"

Now he was awake, and staring at Methos in terror, still trembling. "They—they—"

I wish I could lock that door. "They were dreams," Methos said, forcing his voice to gentleness, "only dreams."

"No!"

"Yes. Remember the ship? Remember back then, when

I told you that these were only dreams, without any power to them?"

"I . . . but . . . yes . . . but . . ."

"I know that they seem dreadfully real to you, but you must believe me, they are nothing more than . . . than so much mist. You are stronger than they, Prince Khyan, remember that. No matter how horrible they may seem, you are always stronger than they. You can stand your ground and defy them, and they will retreat. They will always retreat."

"Yes. Yes!" Khyan grinned, a wide flash of white teeth, and brushed strands of wild hair back from his face. "I *am* stronger! Of course I am."

"Excellent. Now, don't you think you should go back to your chambers before you worry your people?"

A wave of a hand dismissed that thought. "They are but servants. I am a prince."

"And princes, even as common men, need rest. Good night, Prince Khyan."

"Good night."

With immense dignity, the prince stalked away, right into the arms of torch-bearing servants who had, of course, quivering with fear for their own safety, followed their master.

"Don't worry, don't worry," Methos heard the prince say. "It was nothing. Only a dream."

Oh fine, now you realize it.

Khyan vanished into the herd of servants. But one of them, a thin, tense young man, paused, staring at Methos for a long, thoughtful moment.

Aha, our blatant amateur spy!

But when Methos raised an inquisitive eyebrow, the young man's gaze dropped, and he turned and hurried after the prince. Methos stood for a moment more, wondering what had just happened, then gave a sigh that turned into a yawn. Sheathing his sword, he closed the door behind him and sank back to his bed.

Maybe I can get at least some *sleep this night?*

But all the while, his hand never strayed far from the hilt of his sword.

The next disturbance came very early in the morning, before the sky had quite enough color to do more than tell white from black. Methos, nerves still on edge, was awake and on his feet long before the first tentative creaking of the door.

I really must get a lock on that thing!

He waited. A head poked warily inside: Sure enough, it belonged to the young male servant, the would-be spy with the intent gaze. The young man crept carefully into the room—then stopped with a gasp as Methos, slipping behind him, put the edge of his sword tenderly against the youngster's throat.

"Good morning," Methos said in his ear. "Now, do I cut your throat or call for the guards?"

"Neither! Please. I—I just wish to talk with you."

"Feel free."

"Uh . . . if you could just . . . the sword—"

"Why should I move it? How do I know you're not here as an assassin?"

That brought a daring twist of the head so that the young man could glare back at him, and an indignant, "I'm not!"

"No," Methos agreed wryly, lowering the sword. "You're not. No assassin would ever be so clumsy."

He backed off a wary bit, just in case the youngster decided to be dangerous after all. No clothes on the boy save a brief, drab gray kilt, but a long knife was stuck into his belt, and Methos snatched it free, placing it out of the youngster's reach.

"Very well. Turn around, boy. Tell me why you're here."

"You know why!"

"No. I do not. First of all, who are you?"

"My name doesn't matter. I am a—a fighter for our people's freedom!"

Gods, he means it. "How exciting for you," Methos said without expression. "And why are you here, oh Fighter for

Your People's Freedom? For that matter," he added with the smallest touch of sarcasm, "which people might that be?"

The young man stared at him as though he'd suddenly sprouted horns. "Why, the true people, of course! Those on whom the gods of Khemt smile!"

"Ah, in other words, the Egyptians. And you wish to, let me guess, free them from the tyrant's yoke, or words to that effect. Well and good, but why come to me?"

Another horrified stare. "Why, are you not from the pharaoh himself?"

"I came here from Thebes," Methos said carefully. "No more than that."

"But—"

"Boy, listen to me. I am not a secret agent, a spy, an assassin, or any other such dramatic being. If you wish to try overthrowing the evil overlord, that is your affair. Just don't seek to enroll me."

"But you have to help me!"

Save me from idealists! "Boy, freedom fighter, whoever you are, how do I know I can trust you?"

"I swear my honesty by—"

"Yes, yes, oaths are easy. I swear them all the time. That doesn't necessarily mean I believe a word of them. And while we're on the subject, how do you know that *you* can trust *me*? How can you be sure I won't go straight to King Apophis and betray you?"

The boy stared earnestly at him. "You won't. Will you?"

Oh gods, gods, was I ever this naïve? Or this young? "Not if I don't need to do so. Come, tell me, why *are* you here?"

The young man bit his lip, then said in a rush, "To kill King Apophis."

"You don't think small, do you?" Hey now, he was perfectly willing to let the young man assassinate King Apophis: It would certainly make his own job all the easier! "But do you actually have a plan?"

"No one watches servants. I will wait till the king is off

his guard, then rush him! Before anyone can stop me, I'll cut him down!"

"I see. In other words, you don't have a plan." *And as a result, you are far more dangerous than useful.* "Go away, boy. Get yourself killed without my help."

The boy frowned. "I was wrong, wasn't I? You're not a friend of Egypt."

"I'm not its enemy, either."

"No, no, you are a danger to the cause—you will tell the king! I can't allow that!"

He dove for his knife, snatching it up, then lunged. Methos sidestepped, thinking, *Spare me from hotheaded idiots,* caught the boy's arm as he hurtled by, and twisted. The boy went crashing into the door, which flew open, spilling him out into the courtyard. Methos followed, sword drawn—but the youngster had already been seized by two guards, who tore the knife from his hand as he struggled wildly and uselessly.

"Let him go," Methos told them. "This is between the two of us only."

"No!" the young man cried.

"Yes." *You young idiot, shut up! I'm trying to save your life.* "He mistook me for a spy come here to assassinate the king."

But the boy was past the point of logic. "That's not true!" he screamed in an ecstasy of self-sacrifice. "I am the one who meant to kill the king! Freedom for Egypt! Freedom—"

A blow from one guard silenced him. "Thank you, my lord," the other said to Methos. "Be assured, King Apophis shall hear of your courage."

"What of the boy?"

"This one? Oh, he, of course, shall die."

"Of course."

That was, Methos mused, the usual fate of fools. And martyrs.

Which, in his opinion, often came to exactly the same thing.

Chapter Fourteen

Egypt, Avaris: Reign of King Apophis, 1573 B.C.

It wasn't long after the capture of the self-styled freedom fighter that Methos received the predictable second royal summons.

King Apophis, sitting straight-backed and proud on his throne chair in the audience hall, looked as cold as a regal, glittering statue. But as Methos approached at Apophis's beckoning crook of a hand, the king's chill melted into a sort of smile that seemed warm enough even if it didn't quite include his eyes.

"The rebel," Apophis said without preamble, "the would-be assassin, has confessed everything: how he sought to enlist your aid, how you refused him and caused his capture. You have done us a great royal service, Methos. And we shall not forget it."

Conveniently vague wording, that. And thank whatever powers there are that the boy was too stupidly honest to implicate me in anything.

"Kneel," the king commanded.

Warily, Methos obeyed, one foot curled under, ready to spring up or aside should need be. But Apophis did nothing more alarming than set a necklace of gold beads over his head. Methos settled it into place, forcing down a shiver at the touch of the cold metal, telling himself, *This royal token I melt down as soon as I'm out of Avaris!*

"You have aided in the capture of that would-be regicide," King Apophis continued. "And so you shall stand at our side when he is executed in honor of the great god Set."

Oh, joy. Methos bowed. "I shall be honored, King Apophis."

The execution did not take place within the royal chapel—too messy, Methos thought dryly. Too difficult to get bloodstains out of porous marble.

Instead, the prisoner, naked, bloody, and much the worse for wear, was staked out between four pegs hammered into the ground just outside the chapel. His frantic, agonized glance focused on Methos. In a harsh, pain-filled, barely understandable voice, the boy cried:

"May you live forever and never know peace or—"

A blow from a guard's spear haft silenced him.

"Gently," King Apophis warned in a voice that was anything but gentle. "Our god would not wish this traitor too easy a death."

Even if the boy's curse was only the truth, Methos added to himself.

He watched, face carefully impassive, as the prisoner was slowly burned and cut and torn open, slowly disemboweled, slowly turned into so much meat. Methos would not allow himself anything as perilous as pity; he would not allow himself any emotion at all. This was merely something unavoidable to be waited out. Something finite.

Midway through, the screams stopped, as shock mercifully deadened the boy's brain, and Methos bit back a sigh of relief. The prisoner would no longer be aware of much of what was being done to him.

True enough. The boy made not the slightest move as the executioner's blade finally came slashing down. A concerted sigh of satisfaction went up from the assembled courtiers as the executioner held the severed, battered head high. Methos glanced at Khyan to his right and saw nothing but glazed satiety in the prince's eyes, the look of one who has just enjoyed an orgiastic experience.

He is a madman, Methos reminded himself. *He is not to be judged as other men.*

But when he glanced at King Apophis, Methos saw nothing but that same dreadful satiety. The faintest of dreamy smiles was on the royal lips, and for one insane moment, Methos ached to have his sword out and slashing across that royal neck.

I want out of here. I want out of here, now!

It was, of course, a little too late for that.

You got yourself into this perverse lair, and only you can get yourself out again.

He must remember why he was doing this at all. Wasn't the restoration of a happy, stable Egypt worth the risk?

Not particularly. I would much rather keep my head firmly attached to my body. And my entrails, he added as a breeze brought the reek of the execution to him, *where they belong, as well.*

That poor, stupid boy . . . like suicidal Amar back in Albion. What got into boys' heads to turn them into martyrs? Stupid, yes, because once a mortal was dead, he wasn't coming back, and while martyrdom might sound wonderfully self-sacrificing, a dead martyr wasn't half as useful to a cause as a live warrior.

With a start, Methos realized that he was still being watched by both guards and courtiers. *Control,* he told himself. *You feel nothing but satisfaction that a traitor is dead.*

And no one challenged him. He was going to get past this after all.

Was he? Before he could reach his room, a guard overtook him.

"The king wishes to speak with you."

Gods!

"So be it," Methos said, since he could hardly refuse. And his face revealed nothing at all.

This time, the audience chamber held both the king and a good many of King Apophis's aides as well.

I'd want to question me more thoroughly, too. All right, then, let's get this over and done.

King Apophis leaned forward in his throne, smiling. "And now, Methos, we shall discuss the matter of Egypt."

Not about the boy, then! Not an accusation of treason.

What followed was another, even more intensive interrogation, a rapid attack on all sides by the king and his aides.

Naturally. The better to shake my concentration.

It wasn't so easily shaken. Methos had planned for just such an inquisition as this, thanks to having gained insight into the workings of a royal mind over the years. He countered question after question with carefully fabricated answers, slowly and deliberately building up an image of an Egypt utterly demoralized by the death of Pharaoh Sekenenre.

He also, equally carefully, built up the image of a clever man, himself, driven nearly to the edge of despair by frustration.

"At least here," he slipped in as though momentarily overwhelmed by relief, "a man has some scope for his talents!"

"And the new pharaoh?" King Apophis snapped, showing no sign he'd heard.

"Ah, Kamose." Methos paused as though trying to find the most diplomatic way to word what he must say. "He is . . . still young. The young are often . . ." another delicate pause, "impatient."

Apophis and the others would, of course, seek out the double meaning hiding in that, assuming "hot-blooded," which was true, and "stupid," which was not. "And of course, there is also Prince Ahmose," Methos added thoughtfully. "It cannot be easy being a younger brother. And at the same time . . . ambitious."

That Ahmose was also, even so, too fond of his brother to ever consider usurpation was a fact Methos neglected to include. Instead, he continued his deliberate web of insinuation and carefully misinterpreted facts, verbally dueling with the aides, giving King Apophis a great deal of information—little of it true.

Why, I could almost despise myself for a scoundrel—had I not seen that sacrifice. Or rather, King Apophis's enjoyment of it.

It was easy, far too easy, to kill and come to enjoy it. Bad enough. But to find sensual satisfaction in the torture of a boy whose greatest sin was stupid honesty—no. There were, Methos thought, limits.

Ah yes, and limits to questioning, too. The aides were finally falling silent.

Free at last.

But King Apophis snapped without warning, "Are you a spy?"

Methos almost fell into the trap of too strong a denial. Instead, he merely smiled. "As I stated when you asked if I was a magician: If I were, what good to admit it? And if I were not, what good to deny it?"

King Apophis snorted. "And as *I* said, clever. Too clever to be wasted. Go do . . . whatever for now." He did not bother adding the obvious: Don't try to leave Avaris. "I think I will yet find uses for you."

Only in your fancies, King Apophis, only in your fancies.

Methos bowed, received royal permission to leave, and left.

So now. He'd escaped yet another trap. And he had sowed the seeds of misinformation as best as he could. Time now to take advantage of whatever free time he was allowed and feel out the moods at court.

And in the process, look for some weaknesses that just might be exploited.

"Ha, here you are!"

Methos started at the sudden shout and sharp inner warning of another Immortal, then stifled a sigh. The last person he wished to see right now was Prince Khyan.

But before he could make any excuses, Khyan was propelling a warm, soft body full into his arms, saying, laughing, "Here! A gift!"

Methos drew back enough to see that it was, indeed, a woman who had just been all but thrown at him. A young woman, at second glance, though with the air of someone who had suffered so much she no longer cared about youth or even life. Slender, fine-boned, an Egyptian slave, no doubt. What he could see of her lowered head, the sweet curve of a cheek, implied a lovely face, and Methos gently tipped her head up again with a hand—only to force himself not to make the slightest of starts, the slightest sound of surprise.

Her face had, indeed, been lovely. Once. Now the scar of a badly healed burn scored its angry way down one cheek and on down the side of her throat.

"I know she's flawed," Khyan said coarsely, "but not where it matters! Blow out the lamp before you strip her, and you'll find all that a man needs to find! Trust me, it's all there!"

Used goods, and damaged as well.

But there was such dull sadness to the woman that he couldn't mock her, even in thought.

Nor, Methos realized, could he refuse the gift; Khyan would, one way or another, casually kill her, and possibly come after him, too, for the insult.

"I thank you, Prince Khyan," Methos said with a bow. "Woman, come."

"That's right!" Khyan yelled after them. "Try her out! She's a hard worker, that one!"

The woman flinched ever so slightly, and Methos glanced at her. "I won't give you back to him," he said experimentally, and she flashed him a glance of such gratitude that something deep within his being winced.

Oh, I don't need another complication, I really don't.

"Enter," Methos said as they reached his room, and closed the door behind them.

She stood motionless, clearly waiting for the assault.

Methos sighed. "I know what you're expecting, but I, for one, am not in the mood for an attack. Let's take this from step one, shall we? I am Methos. You are . . . ?"

"Whatever you wish to call me, lord."

"Oh no, don't start that! I don't like talking to an image. And I don't think you're a fool, either."

"My lord?"

"You surely have a name. Something your relatives—"

"I have none, lord. None living."

"Ah. Well then, something you call yourself. I am *not* going to name you like a pet!"

That roused the faintest spark of humor in her eyes. Which were, he noted, now that there was a touch of life to them, really rather lovely. And that scar . . . well, it wasn't truly all *that* terrible.

"I am Nebet, Lord Methos."

Her voice wasn't unpleasant, either, low and almost husky. A pity she was a gift from Prince Khyan, and as such probably more dangerous than sweet Tiaa. "And what," Methos wondered aloud, "am I to do with you?"

Her glance was so startled that he gave a short laugh. "Aside from the obvious, that is."

"That is for my lord to decide."

A great deal of simmering hatred lay beneath the docile words. "You were not born a slave," Methos hazarded.

Another startled glance. "No, my lord. I . . . had the misfortune of being in the path of a raid by our noble overlords."

Careful, my dear. That tone bordered on the treasonous. Not that I would betray you. Certainly not to King Apophis. "And is that where you got—where you were injured?"

"No, my lord. That came after."

Something not said made Methos ask, "Prince Khyan?"

Nebet would not quite meet his gaze. "He . . . is touched by the gods, my lord, and does not always see the world as do other men."

"What did he do, Nebet?"

Her voice was too calm, too controlled. "He thought me a demon. And in his horror at the realization, threw the first weapon that came to hand. It was a lighted oil lamp." She shrugged. "I lived."

"I will not return you to him," Methos repeated, and this time meant it.

Nebet said nothing at first. Then, moving to the bed, she asked flatly, "My lord?"

So very easy to take what was being offered—more so since the thought that she dared not resist added a certain spice . . .

No. *There really* are *limits,* Methos told himself sternly. "You don't need to—"

"If my lord does as the prince suggested, extinguishes the lamp, he need not see—"

"Just how cruel do you think me?"

But she could hardly know that, or anything else, about him, so instead of arguing, he moved to her side and very, very gently kissed her. For the barest of instants, it was like kissing a statue. Then her lips softened against his.

When Methos stepped back, Nebet stood, eyes shut. "Did you enjoy that, my lord?"

"What—"

"Did you enjoy it?"

"Yes!"

"Very well." Nebet sat down on the bed, staring up at him without blinking. "Now, my lord, will you please extinguish the lamp?"

"No."

"But, my lord—"

"No, I said! I wish to see what I have here."

She said nothing more, only continued to stare rigidly at him as she stood again, slid her simple gown off her shoulders, and let it pool on the floor. "There, my lord. Does the sight please you?"

The angry red scar continued down her neck, cruelly marring the smooth roundness of one breast as well. But after the first stunned moment, Methos thought as he had before that these were ugly marks, yes, but not so utterly terrible at that. Not so terrible that a sensible, sane man wouldn't see beyond the scars to the loveliness that was still there.

Not all her scars, though, were visible. When Methos, not certain what next step to take, reached out to touch her shoulder, he felt her quickly suppressed shiver. And for a moment he wanted to simply turn and walk away from this new, unwanted problem.

Instead, he said, a little more harshly than he'd intended, "I won't savage you. Dress yourself, woman."

She grabbed at her gown in a spasm of alarm. "You said you wouldn't give me back to him."

"I did. And I won't."

Hastily struggling back into the gown, Nebet moved to his side, touching his arm with a chilly hand, one that almost didn't tremble. "I'm sorry, my lord. I . . . I have known too much brutality."

"I'm not blaming you for your life."

"I know you would be gentle with me; I would like to please you—"

"Nebet," he said, rather surprising himself at the gentleness suddenly in his voice, "I am . . . older than I look, and I've traveled far enough to have seen some truly terrible sights. Those? No."

"My lord . . . ?"

"Those are scars, only that. They may change the way some people—shallow people—look at you, but they only touch part of the surface, not the true Nebet. I think that were conditions more normal . . ."

Methos hesitated, hunting for the proper words, and Nebet finished for him, "Were I not a slave?"

"Precisely. Were that the case, I suspect you'd have had a chance by now to understand what I'm trying to say."

"I think I do. And I think that the . . . scars really aren't so important to you."

"Oh, Nebet! If you'd seen some of the things I've seen—" *And done, over the centuries.* "No," he finished shortly, "they are not."

"And I . . . I think . . ." She paused, as though revealing

anything from behind the psychic wall she'd built about herself was painful.

"Go on. Speak as you will. I won't betray you."

"I think, my lord, that there is more kindness hidden deep within than you would ever admit."

He flinched. "You know nothing about me."

"I know what I've just seen and heard. You could have taken me, yes, or simply thrown me away. Instead . . . Come, my lord." Her hand closed about his, still a little chilly, perhaps, still not quite steady, but decisive in its grip. "Come. Let me learn more of you."

So be it. Gently, as though unwrapping a precious gift, he drew the gown from her body. Lying on his back, relaxed as much as was possible, he let her be the explorer, her hands tentative at first, then more and more certain, wandering over his lean, sleekly muscled self until at last Methos could no longer endure to lie still. Taking her in his arms, he began to make love to her as slowly and carefully as though she were one of those fragile, all-but-transparent alabaster figurines.

But in the middle of it, she caught him fiercely with arms and legs wrapped about him. "I will not break!" Nebet cried. "Love me, my lord, yes! I will not break!"

Eyes open, he saw her face all at once transformed by passion, turned wild and joyous and free, and his heart caught in his throat at this sudden, wondrous, unexpected beauty.

But later, Methos slept with the proverbial one eye open. Not everyone wanted a reminder that there *were* such things as joy and freedom out there beyond a slave's reach. And he was not yet sure if, even after all that tender care, she wasn't going to try knifing him in the dark.

Instead, he realized after a bit that she was silently weeping.

"Nebet?"

No, she was sound asleep. Weeping in her sleep.

"Nebet?" Methos asked again, touching her shoulder. "What is it?"

Her eyes opened. She looked at him blearily, not really quite awake. "Dreaming . . ." Nebet murmured, "was dreaming . . . of happiness."

She fell back into sleep, leaving him staring.

Happiness. The thought that it should be so rare that she would weep over it cut through him like a blade.

You cannot get involved. You must not get involved.

And birds must not fly.

They couldn't, a dark corner of his mind told him, if their wings were cut off.

I should have stayed in Albion. Stupid, suicidal princes or no, I should have stayed in Albion.

Chapter Fifteen

MacLeod glanced at Methos as they made their way down crowded, noisy Third Avenue. "Remembering something?"

"Some*one*," Methos corrected. "Someone, in fact, whom I haven't thought about for . . . well, let's just say for one hell of a long time."

After a few seconds of silence, it became obvious that he wasn't going to volunteer anything more. MacLeod said only a delicately bland, "Some of us, as I've pointed out before, have more to remember than others, Old One."

"And more to consider. Duncan, Young One, this is a city of, what is it now, over eight million?"

Both eyebrows raised at that "Young One," MacLeod agreed, "Something like that."

"Then how do you propose that we find one man, even a man who is one of us, out of all that? Particularly a man the local police, who are far from inefficient, haven't been able to locate?"

But MacLeod's attention was suddenly caught by a flash of motion from a storefront —ah, an appliance store, with a television set turned to . . . "Oh dear God."

Methos joined him at the store window. "Ah. Another killing."

"Another two. Look at that." The news bulletin, with

what MacLeod thought of as ultimate ghoulishness, was showing photographs of two smiling young people, a fresh-faced girl and boy, evidently taken from a school yearbook, superimposed over the murder scene. "What were they? Seventeen, maybe? No more than eighteen. Mortal lives are brief enough, but these two—they didn't even get a chance. What's next, Methos, babies?"

"Ah, and we're blaming ourselves for being Immortal, aren't we? Repeat after me, MacLeod: 'It's not my fault.'"

"It *is* our fault that lunatic's still out there!"

He heard the softest of impatient sighs from Methos. "No. It is not."

On the screen, the angry face of the mayor was speaking into the microphones thrust into his face, clearly raging at the police commissioner: "Why hasn't something been done about this?"

"Something is going to be done," MacLeod said shortly.

"Whoa. Where are you going?"

MacLeod grinned without humor. "Even Young Ones can pick up some wisdom. Where else does one go in this city to do some solid research? To the New York Public Library."

"Oh, of course! We'll just look under Psychotic Killers, comma, Hyksos."

"We'll look," MacLeod said, well aware that Methos had probably already figured out where this was leading, "in the police reports of ritual murders. There has to be some sort of pattern."

"One that the police haven't already noticed?"

"How could they?"

Methos blinked, brought up short. "Ah, good point," he agreed after the briefest of pauses. "How could they possibly know to link the murders to the arrival of one seemingly unspectacular bronze sword in New York? Assuming that said link *is* there, naturally."

"Which the dates on those reports will tell us."

Methos's wave of a hand was melodramatic. "I yield to your youthful wisdom. Lead on."

He had given in, MacLeod thought, with amazing speed. *Almost as though he really had already figured all this out. Or perhaps didn't need to figure it out at all?*

And that absolute callousness . . . granted, Methos had lived so long he must have witnessed every possible aspect of the human psyche. But still . . . the image of that sweet young girl's face . . . how could anyone not be moved by the thought of that poor girl, yes, and her family?

Will I ever grow so utterly indifferent? God no, I refuse to even think that.

But how much might he have already lost of himself in these four hundred years? Yes, and not even have realized it?

I refuse to consider that, as well.

Brave words. But the sense of something not quite right pursued MacLeod all the way down to Fifth Avenue and Forty-second Street. There, an unexpected flash of memory conjured up an image of that site as it had looked a hundred years ago. No handsome Beaux Arts building back then, no steps flanked by those two supercilious stone lions. Back then, there had been only the high walls of the city's main reservoir.

For all I know, Methos remembers this place before anyone built anything at all—assuming that he somehow made it to the New World back in the once-upon-a-time days.

Methos, however, was being his usual enigmatic self, volunteering not a hint. He said nothing as they entered the elegant main hall, nothing as they walked down the echoing marble corridor to the main reference desk. There, MacLeod, pouring on the charm, told the dour young woman behind the desk, "My friend and I are writers researching a recent crime story."

The charm worked enough to force an almost-smile out of her. But she said almost smugly, "Wrong building. You want the Mid-Manhattan branch two blocks south."

As MacLeod and Methos left, Methos still said not a word. Still, MacLeod could almost feel his amusement. But they entered the Mid-Manhattan branch—a solid, more down-to-earth structure than the main building—without further incident. Working their way through a swarm of earnest students and office workers on research missions, MacLeod and Methos made a brief stop just past the main entrance. There, the row of computers that served as electronic directories pointed them in the right direction: Periodicals, second floor.

And in a remarkably short time, the two of them were seated with a mound of recent newspapers and magazines.

Convenient, MacLeod thought. *But then, a great many items in this affair are quickly turning convenient. Maybe even a wee bit too convenient?*

At that thought, MacLeod slammed a book shut with more vehemence than he'd intended. Heads turned and Methos made a startled gesture that could only have been an aborted reach for a sword hilt.

"What," he asked MacLeod, "was that about?"

"Coincidental, isn't it? A little *too* coincidental?"

Methos's face held only a detached amusement. "What is?"

"Oh, nothing much. Just that in this city of over eight million, the one man who has firsthand knowledge of the Hyksos, *and* a Hyksos Immortal the man just happens to have known three thousand years ago, turn up at the same time."

"Coincidences *are* fascinating phenomena, aren't they? Do you know that if Marcus Antonius—that's Mark Antony—"

"I know who he is. Methos, is this some sort of plot? Is this, all of this, part of one of your devious plans?"

Methos's eyes were suddenly utterly cold. "My friend, were I, as you put it, working some vast, intricate plan, I assure you, it would *not* depend on someone as totally unpredictable and unstable as a psychotic murderer."

"Which isn't really an answer."

"No," Methos agreed flatly, "it is not. Now, shall we finish our research?"

Devious as the wind. And as hard to snare. "We shall," MacLeod said, just as flatly.

Thanks to the library's new passion for electronics, those newspapers with earlier dates had already been translated into electronic format. Moving to adjoining carrels, MacLeod and Methos entered into an undeclared race for data. A bemused MacLeod saw, out of the corner of his eyes, Methos's fingers flying over the keyboard with an ease that could only have come with that ten years of researcher practice.

Ah yes, Methos, the Five-Thousand-Year-Old Techie.

And despite his continued edginess, MacLeod had a quick, almost whimsical image of them in the next century or so. Methos would, no doubt, be an expert on some phenomenal new interstellar technology. (And did someone over five thousand years old still anticipate the future? Could he? Or did he just "enjoy the ride"? Who could tell what went on in that mind?)

"Got it," Methos said suddenly, and MacLeod gladly abandoned speculation.

A brief call to the Branson Collection verified the exact date of the Hyksos sword's arrival: April sixteenth.

"And the first ritual slaying," Methos noted, "was April twenty-second."

"Less than a week afterward."

"It *could* be, if you'll pardon the word, coincidence. But I don't think either of us is going to buy that."

"Khyan," MacLeod said.

Methos shrugged. "The evidence is mounting up, isn't it?"

"And there have been four . . . no, five other murders." Checking the records, MacLeod read the dates aloud. "April twenty-ninth, May fifth, May tenth, and May fourteenth." He glanced up. "And last night, of course, was May sixteenth. A shorter and shorter interval between the killings. As though your Khyan were growing desperate."

"He is hardly *my* Khyan. And I don't doubt that he's growing desperate. If he's fallen all the way back to the old

Hyksos ways, I suspect that he's lost track of time and place as well. If that's the case, then all that's truly real to him is the sword."

But then Methos paused, studying MacLeod. "Don't waste pity on the man. Trust me: He doesn't deserve it."

There was absolutely nothing to be read from his face. After an awkward second, both Immortals returned almost with relief to the records and the locations of the killings.

"Seventy-second Street and Riverside Park," MacLeod read. Eleventh Avenue and West Fifteenth Street . . . Fifty-sixth." He glanced up. "Out on a dock, that one; daring of Khyan."

"Probably picked a night when no ships were berthed nearby."

"Probably. Twelfth Avenue and West Fifty-first," MacLeod continued, "Washington and Canal Streets, in the warehouse area. And the latest: Seventy-eighth Street and Riverside Park." He looked up again. "The media got one fact right: All of the killings were at least near the Hudson River."

"Odd, that. Why there?"

"That's what I asked you!"

"No, what I mean is that he knows the sword is here in the city. *How* he knows is something else again: some bizarre instinct, maybe, or some more prosaic news report he's too crazed to remember hearing. I say that because he's also clearly too crazed to zero in on the Branson Collection. But . . . why so specifically the West Side?"

MacLeod shook his head. "You're the Hyksos expert, not me."

"Oh, thank you *so* much. But what would Khyan be attempting? Why, of all the places in this enormous city, the river?" Methos stopped short. "The river—the Nile! Of course, that's it: It's not the park or the West Side he wants, it's the river!"

"I'm not following you. You said that he'd be too insane to locate the sword easily, but—"

"The comparison. The Hudson, broad and powerful as it

is, yes, and even tidal like the Nile, is as close as Khyan can get *to* the Nile. Yes again, and Manhattan Island is as close as Khyan can get to the formation of land on which Avaris once stood—he must be blessing Set for the similarity!"

"I almost hate to bring this up," MacLeod cut in, "but even if it is Khyan out there, that's a good eight miles of riverfront. The police are going to be on the lookout for the West Side Slayer, particularly with the mayor *and* the media after them, but they can't patrol all that expanse all the time."

"Neither," Methos pointed out, "for the same reason, can we." He paused thoughtfully. "There has to be some clue, though . . . something I can remember about him."

But after a time of silence, Methos shook his head. "Nothing. Nothing useful, at any rate. Ah well, I think we've learned all we can here."

MacLeod glanced up at the time. "We'll make copies of the pertinent pages, then go get some lunch."

"Good idea. Maybe coffee will give my brain a proper jolt."

There were at least a dozen coffee shops nearby, crowded with office workers grabbing the usual quick lunches. Over sandwiches and coffee, his words nearly drowned out by the chatter and bustle around them, MacLeod asked Methos a wary, "Well?"

"Well what? I can tell you pretty much what Avaris looked like, why you didn't go swimming in the Nile—crocodiles—and what the ladies were wearing, or not wearing, more precisely, in Egypt's Sixteenth Dynasty. What more do you want?"

"Can't you remember *anything* about Khyan? Any quirks we could use, any weird little habits or weaknesses?"

"MacLeod, I'm not a computer!"

"Yes, but you were there— All right, let's try to be logical about this. Why *does* he want the sword?"

Methos shook his head. "Two possibilities. I'd guess he

either wants to free the captured soul or else keep it with him forever."

"What would that mean? What sort of ritual?"

"I don't know! I wasn't exactly a student of the occult." A shrug. "Something bloody, probably."

"Something worse than we've got now? Are we talking about a massacre?"

"I don't *know!*"

"Don't keep saying that!"

"And can *you* really recall everything about everyone you ever met?" Methos countered. "Try living five thousand years, and see how sharp *your* memories stay!"

MacLeod suspected that, for all his denials, Methos's memories were sharp enough. Getting to his feet, he said, "Let's go for a walk."

"Eh?"

"In Riverside Park."

"The sight of the Hudson just may be jogging loose some Nile memories?" Methos shrugged. "It's worth a try. Right now I haven't got any better ideas."

"Now there's a first." That earned him a wry glance from Methos. "Who knows?" MacLeod continued. "We might even be lucky enough to surprise Khyan in the act."

"Oh, I doubt that!"

"Life not being so, ah, coincidental, right? Well then, at the very least, my skeptical friend, we'll still accomplish one thing."

"And that being . . . ?"

MacLeod forced a grin. "We'll get us some exercise."

Chapter Sixteen

====

Egypt, Avaris: Reign of King Apophis, 1573 B.C.

Methos lay awake, Nebet a warm weight against his chest, his arm around her and her unbraided hair spread sleekly across them both. The first faint light of early morning filtered down from the high windows near the ceiling, smoothing her scars, making her face truly young again, young and innocent. Smiling faintly, Methos raised a hand to stroke her hair.

Oh no, he warned himself, lowering that hand again. *You are not going to start this. Just because she is a wounded dove, or whatever metaphor they're using here these days, you are not going to start playing healer. Or anything more sentimental.*

He carefully disentangled himself from her, went in search of the terse Hyksos equivalent of sanitary facilities, then returned to begin his morning exercises (even though an unruly part of his mind was clamoring for more pleasant exertion).

Methos was engrossed in the pattern of the sword, cut up, cut left, right, defend, lunge, when he suddenly realized that Nebet was awake and watching him from the bed. He said nothing, intent on bringing the pattern to its proper conclusion. Only then did he turn to her.

"Beautiful," she murmured.

He shrugged. "I am, among other things, a warrior. The

sword demands daily practice, and I agree, the proper moves probably do look like a dance or—"

"I wasn't referring to the sword," Nebet cut in, then gave the softest, most delicious of laughs. "Why, my lord, I didn't know you could blush!"

"Huh." Sheathing the blade, Methos put it aside. "Nebet, much as I would love to stay and, ah, discuss standards of beauty with you, I'm afraid that I have less aesthetic matters to attend."

"Never fear, my lord. I will be here when you return."

The thought sent a little shock of delight through him.

Gods, what a fool you are. After all these years, what a sentimental fool!

Without another word, he dressed and left to explore what he could of the fortress.

It wasn't as much as he would have liked. Too many areas were blocked by guards who said, "Forbidden." As for getting out into the town beyond the fortress walls: "Forbidden."

Damnation.

Those sections of the fortress through which he was allowed to wander looked more and more impregnable every time he studied them: thick walls everywhere, and no way to undermine them without being cut down by the guards always present in those cursed watchtowers.

What of the court? Methos wondered, and set his mind to them.

In the next few days, he walked warily, insinuating himself so delicately into conversations that no one objected to his presence, saying almost nothing, staying so still that courtiers grew careless and spoke freely.

And even so, maddeningly, they gave away nothing much.

I really don't care that Salitis spread rumors about Ketys and his mistress, or that Yakobaan and Sheshi may be more than, nudge, wink, good friends. You get that type of backbiting and spite in any royal court.

The point was that, for all the discontent, even that

aimed at the king, there seemed to be little anti-Apophis unity. Methos overheard Salitis, the rumormonger, a lean, wiry fellow who looked like one of those Egyptian hunting hounds, a saluki, and Sheshi, who just might be more than friends with Yakobaan but looked more like a bull than, as the rumor put it so delicately, a cow.

"Yes," Sheshi snapped, "but he wastes too much time on that half-brother."

"Exactly! Our king should be taking more wives, getting us an heir."

Mortals, Methos mused dryly, just didn't always get the idea of what "sterility" meant, or even that a king might be so unfortunately afflicted.

"An heir," Sheshi snorted. "Right now all we have is that lunatic."

"If King Apophis dies, which Set prevent," Salitis added, both men making a quick warding-off-evil sign, "how long do you think Prince Khyan's going to reign?"

"Or," Sheshi added softly, "live?"

Methos carefully insinuated himself into the conversation. "There is a saying," he commented to no one in particular, "that the barrenness of the king may cause the barrenness of the land. Odd, isn't it?"

Sheshi snorted. "Who cares about this land?"

Then the subject changed to generic warfare, and boasting about killings and conquests, and Methos wandered on. With the next group, he commented, "There is an odd belief in this land: The barrenness of the land reflects itself on the king."

"An Egyptian belief!"

"Why should we believe anything a conquered people claim?"

Again, Methos wandered on. There had been a good many exchanges along these lines from other courtiers. While that "sterility of king equals sterility of land" and its corollary might have worked elsewhere, the Hyksos weren't particularly interested in the well-being of a land they had merely conquered, and failed to believe that land could ever prove a threat.

Foolish of them, since they survive off what the land they so scorn produces. By the time they managed to import sufficient food from Palestine, and assured never-ending quantities, they'd all have starved to death.

It wasn't the first time he'd come across such a short-sighted view. Such a mortal view.

And as for King Apophis, unfortunately for rebellion, he was such a strong, vigorous man that no one was accepting that, as the saying went, his quiver might be empty.

A stifled scream cut into his thoughts. Methos saw a young man, a slave, huddled on the floor, hands over his face, blood seeping through his fingers. Sheshi stood over him, calmly wiping a dagger clean on the slave's hair.

"My lord Sheshi," Methos began, thinking, *Foiled assassination.* "What happened?"

With a bored gesture, Sheshi indicated the shattered pieces of jar. "He was clumsy. Ugly and clumsy," he added, bending to catch the slave's hair in his hand and drag back his head. "I've just improved his looks. No, slave, don't hide your face, lower your hands. Let the lord see."

"I see," Methos said flatly. Beneath the mask of still-flowing blood, it was clear that the slave's nose had been slit open. "Of course now the slave has been rendered useless until he has healed."

Sheshi shrugged. "There are always others."

Nebet.

No, don't think of her. She is safe enough: No one will harm Khyan's royal gift.

With a curt bow, Methos went on before he said or did something reckless. There were all too many of these casual cruelties in a court filled with bored warrior nobles. Just the other day, he'd seen Salitis slowly, lovingly flogging a female slave merely to, as he'd put it, test out a new whip.

Gods, I despise these people! And, curse them, it's grow-ing more and more difficult to hide that fact.

It was all the more difficult since Methos by now was often a part of court proceedings, advising the king—along with, of course, a good many Hyksos advisors. He was al-ways scrupulously honest at such times; it was too risky to the image of utter usefulness he was crafting to be other-wise.

But being honest meant guarding one's tongue against too much honesty! After so many years of existence, no Immortal could be squeamish or particularly finicky. It was only common sense and good politics to kill an enemy, a rebel, or would be regicide, even, yes, to torture him to death.

We all have some darkness within us. But a civilized people have boundaries!

As these folk, bored and vicious, did not.

Yet what could one man, even one Immortal, do about it? Granted, there *was* a certain challenge here. But there was a more important challenge—namely, that of keeping his head!

Methos was still pondering the problem early the next morning, idly toying with a lock of Nebet's hair, she a warm, sleepy softness at his side.

So now, he mused, thinking of the court. *Time to retreat and regroup. I'm not going to foment rebellion with that lot, or corrupt Apophis, as it were, to the ways of niceness.*

But there was another course, Methos knew: He could make friends, if he could stomach it, with Prince Khyan. It would be as perilous a course as it was unpleasant. With someone walking as fine a line between sanity and chaos as the prince, there was always the danger of saying or doing something wrong. One mistake, and Methos knew he could very well spark Khyan's madness and smoldering sadism against *him.*

But such a friendship would be my key into the forbid-

den corners of Avaris. Then, with any luck, I can find the fortress's flaw and get out of here.

Persuade them to let me out of here, he corrected.

Persuade them, he corrected yet again, *to let me and Nebet out of here.*

"Nebet," Methos said softly, and then more forcefully, "Nebet!"

She stirred, eyes opening. "My lord." It was a purr.

"Morning, Nebet. Time to rise."

A chuckle. "Yes, my lord."

And her hand stole smoothly down his chest, down his flat stomach, aiming for . . .

Methos's laugh came out as a gasp. "Just what I needed: a double meaning."

"Just a literal mind. Your wish is my law, my lord," she said, then gave a little shriek of a laugh as he rolled over, pinning her to the bed, her slim golden body, strong from years of slave labor, writhing deliciously beneath him.

A corner of Methos's mind noted that when he'd first bedded her, only the few short nights ago, she would never have tolerated being caught like this. She had so quickly come to trust him. Odd thought, disturbing thought, and to banish it, he kissed her eyelids, her nose, her mouth. . . .

Maybe they didn't have to get up just yet after all.

The sudden blaze warning of another Immortal shot through him, even as a voice outside the room yelped, "Methos! Hey in there, Methos!"

Methos groaned and rolled back over onto his back. "I am going to kill him. Prince or no, I really am going to kill him."

Nebet stared at him in horror. "No, my lord! They would kill you!"

"Mmm. I don't die that easily. It was a jest, Nebet," he added, running a finger down the line of her cheek. "Just a jest."

She drew back. "You mustn't joke, not of that. My lord, there is no escape from Avaris, not unless you are granted passage. Don't you think I know that? I have seen what they do to slaves who make the attempt. Believe me, my lord, I have considered the only other escape, dying by my own hand, letting the gods judge me. But I . . . lack the courage."

"For which, my dear, I am truly grateful."

"You don't understand! Without a pass, the only other way out of Avaris *is* through death. And I . . . I have seen how they punish those who kill—"

"No one. I am killing no one, Nebet."

"Methos!" came the shout from outside.

Methos wearily got to his feet, stretching. "Yes, Prince Khyan. I'll be with you shortly."

Another day, another chance for knowledge.

Another hope of getting out of here.

Methos turned back to Nebet, who was pulling on her single gown. "When I leave," he said, "you will go with me."

She only nodded.

"Didn't you hear me, Nebet?"

"My lord, I did. But don't make promises you can't keep."

"I will keep this one. Trust me. I will set you free."

"My lord, I have chores to do. And Prince Khyan is waiting for you."

She would say nothing more, and Methos gave it up, hastily wrapping his kilt about his waist and slipping his feet into his sandals, then leaving the room.

Khyan was, indeed, waiting, and looking disgustingly hearty. "So, there you are! I should never have given you that woman; she takes up too much time!"

A dangerous topic. "Had I known you were looking for me, Prince Khyan," Methos said smoothly, "I never would have kept you waiting. We two who are touched by the gods have too much in common."

"True, true." Khyan paused. "I need to speak with you. Privately."

"Of course." *Does the chapel of nasty Set count, I wonder,* he thought sardonically, *as Holy Ground?*

But Khyan was catching him by the arm, propelling him along. "The dreams," the prince murmured, and suddenly his heartiness was replaced by the shyness of a frightened child. "You told me that they could not harm me."

"And so they cannot!"

But then Methos stopped short, thinking quickly. Useless to tell the prince, *They're all in your head.* You did not tell the insane they *were* insane. You did not remove all hope.

"There are demons," Methos told Khyan gently. "We both know that. And they envy you."

"They . . . envy me?"

"Why, yes! You have your brother's love—and what demon can make claim to any love? Here is what you must do, Prince Khyan."

"Fight them?"

"No," Methos said hastily, thinking of how Nebet had been injured. "No. Mock them. No matter how terrible the dreams may seem, no matter how terrible the demons, if you laugh at them, you conquer. They cannot bear your laughter."

"Splendid, splendid!" Khyan's slap on the back nearly staggered Methos. "Laugh at them like the foolish things they are—yes! We are alike, we two. And I am glad that when my brother wanted to kill you, I told him no!"

I didn't know there had been such a discussion! Quickly covering, Methos forced a grin. *Friendship,* he reminded himself, *build friendship.* "So am I, Prince Khyan, so am I. Come, let us walk together."

And let me not kill you, either.

Yet.

Chapter Seventeen

Egypt, Avaris: Reign of King Apophis, 1573 B.C.

They lay in drowsy contentment, Methos and Nebet curled up together by flickering candlelight, somewhere in the small hours of the night.

"Now I know how Isis felt," Nebet murmured, "if such a thought is not sacrilegious. Now I know how she felt, divine lady, with her beloved Osiris. Even death could not separate them."

"I know." The Egyptians believed that after Set had murdered his brother, Isis had restored Osiris to life, though he could only remain so in the Afterworld, where he reigned supreme. "And Horus, their son, defeated Set. Nebet, this is strange talk for the middle of the night."

"No, no, you don't understand! For us, for the Egyptians, life is the thing, stronger than any death. And so our Afterworld is but Egypt's life continued, with no grief, no harm, nothing but joy."

"I know that, and it sounds charming. But I'm not quite ready to visit it, thank you. Assuming," he added with a chuckle, "that your Osiris would ever allow me in there!"

"Hush, my lord. Hush. The gods hear all."

"Then why do they—"

She silenced him with a kiss that was more soothing than passionate, then settled herself back to sleep.

Methos, still awake, smiled to himself, in this moment of privacy for once allowing true warmth to show. Could he have only known Nebet for merely a month? Such an incredibly short time! A month of seeing her turned to warm silver by moonlight or washed in bright gold sunlight. A month of watching her move, so wonderfully graceful even when merely carrying a water bucket, of watching her bloom, learning her hopes, her dreams, finding the warm, witty, tender woman who had been hiding behind the safe, dull mask of "I don't feel."

One small month, and yet, it already felt strangely as though she'd always been here, in his room, in his bed, in his life—

Gods, you're not going to get maudlin about it!

Nebet murmured in her sleep, cuddling up against him, and Methos sighed. Controlling his mind was simple; not so easy to control the rest of him.

Lovely, though, truly lovely, to be, for however briefly, at peace: no Immortal nearby, no Game, no lunatic prince out for who knew what weirdness. Just now he could pretend with all his heart that he was no more than one ordinary man in bed with a woman he . . .

But Methos stopped just short of that perilous word "love."

Nebet suddenly stirred, awake again, and gave the softest of chuckles.

"What?" he asked.

"Nothing, my lord."

"Nebet, I told you, in this room you may speak freely and frankly. What?"

"Merely that I never expected this. I thought my emotions as dead as my village, but they were not. I thought them burned away when . . . when Prince Khyan threw that oil lamp. But again, they live."

"For which I am grateful," he added, tapping her gently on the nose with a forefinger.

She turned onto her side to study him. "I should hate you."

"I beg your pardon?"

"I *wanted* to hate you."

"Why?"

"For being free, for being . . . unmarred." Her voice faltered. But then Nebet continued flatly. "I had built up a wall about me. So no one could touch me. Hurt me. I wanted to hate you because you tore it down. I started feeling again. Caring. You saw me too clearly, the true, inner me."

Her expression softened, and she rested a hand on his cheek for a moment before continuing, "But I cannot hate you. Whatever happens next, whatever the gods bring, at least I have had this time with you."

He hoisted himself up on one elbow. "Hey now, no need to speak of us in the past tense. There are still things that we can do together."

His fingers began to trace a delicate path down her body, strolling lightly down her breast, her belly, and Nebet laughed and caught his hand before it could go any lower.

"Yes, we can," she purred. "We can, indeed."

"Methos! My lord Methos!"

Methos woke with a start at the autocratic shout sounding from just outside his room and the warning blaze that an Immortal was near, and was up and out of the bed in an instinctive instant, sword in hand. Behind him, Nebet, dislodged from her comfortable curling against him, murmured something incoherent and unhappy, eyes resolutely shut. Gods, what time was it, still the middle of the night?

No, judging from the dim light, it was the merest dawning of the new day.

"My lord Methos!"

With a sigh that wasn't really of relief, Methos sheathed his sword. "Doesn't the man ever *sleep*? No, don't answer that; idle question. Prince Khyan," he called out in resignation, "I'll be with you in a moment."

Yawning, Methos hastily wrapped a linen kilt about his waist and ran a hand through his hair. Good enough.

Nebet, now more or less awake, looked blearily up at

him from the bed, hair fallen half over her face. "Must you?"

"If I don't, he'll come bounding in here like an eager hound." Methos bent to give her a quick kiss. "Till later, my dear."

Sure enough, the prince was waiting just outside the door, clearly on the verge of bursting into the room. "Ah, here you are! Here you are!"

He lunged. For one stunned moment, Methos, with no idea of what he'd done wrong, was sure it was an attack. But then he realized that all Khyan meant to do was embrace him.

All?

"It worked!" the prince yelled.

"I'm delighted to hear that. But if I may ask, *what* worked?"

Khyan drew back with a frown, then laughed. For all Methos's attempts to dodge without making it look as though he *were* dodging, he still couldn't avoid the prince, who dropped a companionable arm across his shoulders. Trying not to stagger under the unwelcome weight, Methos thought as he had with ever-increasing frequency lately, *I'm going to kill him. One of these days I am going to kill him.*

And get himself killed in the process? What could not be changed, Methos reminded himself, must be endured. And at least the prince did seem to have wholeheartedly adopted him as a friend.

"Methos, it did work!" Khyan all but shouted in his ear, and at last explained. "The demons in the night—I wouldn't let them frighten me. No, no, I laughed at them—and they vanished into mist and let me be! Just the way you told me, I mocked them, and they vanished!"

"Excellent." *For the moment. Until your disturbed mind forgets this and we must begin all over again.*

For three days now, they had gone through a similar process, Methos carefully wooing the prince, helping him out of the morass of his dreams—only to have Khyan forget from one moment to the next.

"Now you must come, hurry," the prince added, "to attend the rites of Set."

Methos, smothering another yawn and edging ever so subtly out from under the royal arm, asked, "Isn't it a bit early for, ah, regular services?"

The hearty camaraderie vanished from Khyan's face in a flash. "Do you question me?"

"Of course not, Prince Khyan!" Methos said smoothly. "It's merely that, as a newcomer to this court, I sometimes do display my ignorance."

"Ah, of course, of course. I forget that you have not been here forever, you and I, the two touched by the gods." Khyan paused, smiling slyly. "That would be the future, you and I, the guardians of the realm, the rulers of the world, you and I, touched by the gods and gods ourselves."

"It . . . would be intriguing," Methos said warily, knowing better than to try to follow Khyan's convoluted reasoning.

"Intriguing," Khyan said with a laugh. "That is what is wrong with you, Methos. You think small. Listen: I love my brother, I wish him ever, ever well. You know that. You do know that!"

"Prince Khyan," Methos told him with absolute honesty, "there is no love more unique than that between you and your brother." *For any other king would have had such a liability as you eliminated long ago.*

Khyan, of course, took it for a compliment. "True, true. But—ah, look. The guards are practicing their swordplay. We shall join them."

So much for the rites of Set. Not that I regret missing them.

But he didn't want to get caught up in more swordplay, either. "Prince Khyan," Methos began carefully, "I wonder if I might ask a kindness of you." *Now, while we are still good friends.*

"I know, you want a different woman. An unflawed one!

I jested in giving the scarred one to you. Come, you shall pick another!"

"That's not necessary."

"I said, you shall pick another!"

"Prince Khyan, I would not deign to deny your royal kindness. But I . . . I am a humble man. I would not feel at home with too, ah, rich a diet."

A pause. Then Khyan gave a sharp bark of a comprehending laugh and slapped Methos on the arm. "Indeed, indeed! Too rich a diet can kill a man, and I do not wish you killed!"

Very delicately, Methos asked, "But . . . the favor?"

"You wish something? Ask."

"I have seen some of the splendor of your brother's court"—*oh, indeed, if thick fortress walls, imitations of Egyptian frescoes, and the occasional pretty piece of Canaanite pottery can be considered splendor*—"but only some. Surely there are more wonders? And what of the town? Shall there not be wonders to be seen there, too?"

Khyan frowned. "You cannot go alone. Ha, but I shall go with you! Come."

He led Methos on a complicated, irrational tour of palace, town, palace, garden, town, all the while keeping up a running monologue of hopes and fears and dreams, none of them rational, either. Methos nodded when appropriate, added phrases of comfort or approval from time to time, and all the while noted everything around him.

The outer walls: just as impermeable as those of the citadel. Methos saw merchants and waterbearers in wagons or on foot coming into the city only after rigorous searches by the guards, the other merchants leaving only after undergoing similarly thorough searches.

No smuggling of anyone in or out. Well, I thought not.

In Khyan's erratic company, he wandered the marketplace, seeing some handsome weavings and ceramics, some handicrafts in gold or bronze. The people seemed an edgy, grim-faced lot. Even so, Methos stopped in unexpected pleasure to listen to a talented harper with a many-stringed instrument foreign to Egypt—only to have Khyan take him by the arm and pull him impatiently away.

"Those are common things, unworthy of our time," the prince said with an aloof wave of his hand. "There are better things to see. And we have some most important issues to discuss."

"Forgive my ignorance, but: We do?"

"Yes! About the future and the ruling of the world!"

And we are off and running through a fantasy realm once more, Methos thought wearily.

Were they? In the middle of the marketplace, Khyan stopped short and said suspiciously and utterly without preamble, "Do you love her?"

It caught Methos by surprise. "Her?"

"The slave! The marred one! Do you love her?"

Jealousy? Too strong a denial would be as risky as an admittance. "She's a slave," Methos said in an absolutely neutral voice. "What is that to me? Do you want her back? I would—"

"No, no," Khyan cut in, predictably. "She is a gift. What do you think of this dagger, eh? Worthy of a prince?"

Methos gave an inward sigh of relief. Khyan had dropped the subject of Nebet so suddenly that it was clear his mind had already abandoned it.

And I am not about to remind him.

Back into the fortress. Back through a maze of insanity. And all the while, Methos pretended, as he had been pretending for what seemed an eternity now, to be fascinated by Khyan's weird visions, listening to him boast about being a prince (conveniently forgetting his lack of royal blood), hearing all the dreams that could never come true. And all the while, Methos managed to never once say the undeniably suicidal things that were on his mind.

He was almost relieved when King Apophis called for him.

To his surprise, though, this was not a royal audience. "Walk with me," the king commanded, and every one of Methos's survival instincts came alert and wary.

Guards followed them down the fortress corridors, but at a discreet distance, granting them the illusion of privacy.

"I am in a difficult position," Apophis said without warning. "I need not tell you that even after a hundred years of occupation, we still do not truly *own* Egypt. And I cannot afford even the smallest of weaknesses or, shall we say, liabilities." He glanced shrewdly at Methos. "I don't think I need to spell out the details."

"Your Majesty, might we be speaking about one who has been . . . ah . . . touched by the gods?"

"My brother, you mean. Indeed." After a moment, the king continued, "I could wish he were *not* touched by the gods. But the great god Set is, after all, a deity of chaos. And who are mortal men to argue with that? Khyan is as he is. And I do love him; I have since the days when he was a small boy waking in terror from one of his dreams and only I could comfort him. Now . . . I cannot keep eternal watch over him."

In other words, oh king, you are looking to me to take your beloved, troublesome brother off your hands. Yes, and grateful to me for what I've already done, though that you will never say.

Methos, wisely, said only an innocuous, "One does what one can."

"Yes."

As though suddenly impatient with himself for having revealed anything of himself, the king turned away. "Keep him from harm." He added with a gesture of dismissal, "You have our leave to go."

Methos went.

But he stopped at the edge of the central courtyard at the sound of men's shouts. That was most notably Khyan's voice rising over the others.

And that is Nebet he has cornered!

Methos broke into a run, just in time to see Khyan's men cut off her escape and Khyan grab her, laughing. Nebet, struggling with the ferocity of someone with nothing left to lose, snaked her head down and bit him on the hand. The prince released her with a yelp of startled pain. A savage backhanded slap sent Nebet staggering right into Methos's arms.

"What," he asked mildly, "is happening here?"

Khyan, sucking the hand that Nebet had bitten—though, of course, any toothmarks were already healing—said, "I *told* you that one was damaged. I was just getting rid of it for you, getting you a new one."

Methos felt Nebet tense, but he tightened his grip on her arms, hard enough to make her wince but keep silent. "That is very kind of you," he told Prince Khyan. "But, do you know something?" Methos chucked Nebet under the chin. "I've just gotten this one nicely broken in."

He gave Nebet a kiss so savage it bordered on an attack, hearing the catcalls of Khyan's men.

Khyan wasn't laughing. "She bit me," he muttered. "She assaulted the royal presence."

Gods, that's probably a beheading offense around here.

"Don't worry," Methos said with a fierce grin. "She will be punished."

More catcalls at that, some cries of, "Let us help!"

Only Khyan, disconcertingly, still showed no sign of humor. But then, without warning, he began to laugh as a child laughs, far too loudly, mouth too wide. He was still laughing as Methos, trying not to shudder at the insane sound, dragged Nebet away.

Once they were behind the relative safety of the closed door of his room, Methos released her, asking, "Are you all right?"

Khyan's slap was still blazing red across her too-pale face, livid as the scars, but she nodded.

"Then what," Methos asked with great restraint, "happened?"

"More or less what you saw." Her voice was infinitely weary. "Khyan and his men surprised me. I thought it was just the usual games. But then Khyan said that I was not worthy of you. And I—I discovered to my surprise that I still very much wanted to live." She gave a bitter little laugh. "And so, by fighting to live, I have most probably condemned myself to death."

"No. You have not. Not if I can keep our crazed prince believing I'm his savior."

"Methos, my lord, I know something of that—no, no, I know you haven't told me, but I have eyes, ears. You can't go on playing this dangerous game!"

"Believe me, this isn't my idea of any sort of game. But so far I haven't found any vital clue . . . not with those strong walls, those sturdy guard towers—"

He stopped short, staring at Nebet. "What are you doing?"

"My lord?"

"What are you doing?"

"Why, nothing, my lord, merely seeing if the water in the washbasin is—"

"The water!" Methos exploded.

"My lord?"

"Water, yes, of course, water! And no, Nebet, I have not gone mad. Good gods, woman, the clue was so obvious it was practically slapping me in the face!"

"I don't—"

"I saw it, I saw the waterbearers coming into Avaris, and didn't even realize. Nebet, do you know of any wells in this fortress? Anywhere in the town outside?"

Wondering, she shook her head.

"What about springs?"

"I don't know; I don't have the freedom of the entire enclave."

"Then I'll need to examine Avaris again myself. But, curse me for a too-clever fool, I think I may have found exactly what I needed to know." He caught her by the shoulders. "I don't want to leave you unguarded. Stay at my side, Nebet. Follow me about like a dutiful slave."

"I cannot."

"But—"

"My lord, that isn't the custom, a woman slave following her master in public. And we both know that any breach of custom is only going to attract attention. More, I think, than either of us wishes. Don't fear, my lord," she added with a smile. "I'll be safe enough here."

"Maybe," Methos said warily. "I don't *think* the prince is going to remember his anger for very long. But you must stay out of his sight. The risk to you—"

"My lord Methos, I have survived this long in this place by being cautious; I will survive a little longer." But then she added with a wry little smile, "Now that I know you, my lord, I do, indeed, wish to live."

"Nebet, I . . ."

But, overwhelmed by what he saw in her eyes and utterly astonished at himself, Methos could find nothing else to say.

Why here? Why now? And why oh why, oh gods of utter farce, with her?

And why not ask the lightning why it strikes while you're at it? Methos answered himself scornfully, and left.

The sooner he proved his theory to himself, the sooner he could safely get them both out of here.

Chapter Eighteen

Egypt, Avaris: Reign of King Apophis, 1573 B.C.

Methos bided his time with an Immortal's patience, not wanting to attract attention with any sudden activity. When he finally did stroll out and about Avaris, allowed a little more freedom now as Khyan's friend, it was as a man seemingly at total ease. And, sure enough, no one really paid much visible heed—though Methos was very well aware that he was still being watched.

Ignore them. You are merely a bored man wandering about without the slightest harm in mind. Just looking here . . . and here . . .

He spoke amiably with a few people, seemingly at random, asked a few apparently innocuous questions, none of which could be put together into a treasonous whole by any spy, then wandered about a bit more—and all the while missed not a single detail of the citadel or town.

And at last the evidence both of his own eyes and of the words of the people to whom he'd spoken seemed undeniable.

It's true: a weakness so obvious that they all missed it.

In all this fortress, this vast, powerful fortress, in all the town crowded behind that so-threatening wall, there is not one source of fresh water!

Nebet would, no doubt, be as astonished at the discovery as he.

But when he returned, Methos found his room strangely

empty, with the undeniable feel not of a temporary absence but of true removal.

Refusing to worry, Methos stopped a passing slave, a thin, weary-eyed man. "Where is Nebet? I have need of her."

The slave would not meet his gaze. "Forgive me, my lord. I—I have not seen her."

"Now here's a funny thing: I don't think that you're telling me the truth."

The slave shivered, one uncontrollable convulsion. "My lord, please . . ."

"Am I asking so difficult a question? Let me repeat it. Where. Is. Nebet?"

"My lord, forgive me, but I . . . have been told that . . . there is no one by that name."

Never panic, Methos warned himself. *Show nothing more than the mildest of interest.* "Now that," he said casually, "we both know is a lie. A pity, because the woman is an agreeable convenience." Just as casually, Methos caught the slave by the bony shoulders. "And now you will tell me the truth."

The slave made one token attempt at escape, then sagged in surrender. "My lord, forget that one," he murmured. "She has been taken as a traitor."

Khyan.

It was useless to go after that lunatic. Releasing the slave so suddenly that the man nearly fell, Methos instead went in search of King Apophis.

Allowed into the royal presence with alarming ease, Methos warily began a careful web of mostly truth, observations of Avaris, touching on a warning of poor morale, making it seem a very real report by a man trying to establish a place at court.

"Incidentally, oh king," he added casually, "speaking of morale, my personal slave seems to have gone missing."

King Apophis smiled ever so thinly. "For a newcomer to Avaris, you do seem to have become a focal point for treason."

Ah. "Your pardon, but I don't see—"

"Have no fear. Were I accusing you, you would already be joining the little fool as part of the rites of Set."

"The slave? King Apophis, I know that she was foolish enough to struggle against Prince Khyan, but I had considered that matter settled."

"Really? Then you will be stunned to learn that the woman was part of the plot to assassinate me."

"Impossible!" Methos burst out in the tone of a man too stunned to be careful. "King Apophis, I—she—I couldn't have been so wrong about her, she couldn't—"

"She was as false as that young fool we sacrificed."

In Apophis's eyes was the satisfaction not of catching a spy in a trap but of seeing a clever man discomfited, and Methos realized, *This is your doing. Not just to keep your brother content but to give my loyalty a final test. Ah, Nebet...*

"But she—was she put to the question?" he asked, the stammering quite genuine. "Was she working alone? King Apophis, is there a wider conspiracy? Gods, I slept with her—she could have killed me!"

Careful, careful, a wary corner of his mind warned, the creation you've built up wouldn't grow hysterical.

True enough. Methos took a deep, deliberate breath. "King Apophis, if there is anything that I may do—"

"The affair will be settled."

"Your pardon, oh king, but there was some insult to me, too. Give me the chance to avenge myself."

The king studied him for a long, thoughtful while. Methos stared right back at him, face set in the cold mask that revealed nothing but ruthlessness. "Would you do that? Are you that harsh a man?"

Methos let not the slightest trace of expression cross his face. "I am what I am."

"So now! Yes, you shall attend, and participate. And I am sure that you will not fail me. Come."

Now?

For one insane moment, Methos thought of grabbing Nebet and cutting their way out of Avaris.

Out of this monstrosity? Oh, indeed. And then I'll mount a horse with wings and fly us away.

There was, he knew with brutal honesty, nothing that he could do for her. Nothing.

Except . . .

I promised to set her free, Methos thought bitterly. And that, Nebet, that I shall do.

At least she had not been tortured. There had not been time for it.

Yet. As Nebet was stripped, refusing to show any sign of humiliation or even awareness of her surroundings, then was staked out on the ground, Methos could feel the rising tide of sadistic lust rising from the men around him. Torture there would be, he knew that, and it would not be so much in punishment or for information, but for no other reason than that the target was female and helpless.

He watched the implements of torture set out with care and saw Khyan lovingly fingering a barbed whip.

Sorry to disappoint you all, Methos thought.

With one swift lunge, he snatched a sword from the nearest guard. Instantly, the others drew theirs as well—but Methos was not about to try any one-against-many suicide. His gaze locked with that of Nebet. Her eyes warm, she nodded once, understanding. A wave of quick memories stormed through him: Nebet laughing, Nebet tenderly touching his cheek, Nebet curled up beside him, warm and loving—oh gods, gods, to lose her now when they had just found each other, to be cheated of all the many joyous possibilities—

I vowed to set you free! Methos thought wildly. I keep that vow!

And he brought his sword flashing down in one quick, deadly, merciful blow.

Unable to look at what he'd just done, Methos whirled

to King Apophis, letting all his rage and anguish out in one roar:

"We are avenged!"

Gods, oh gods, if only he could attack, cut down Apophis, behead Khyan—

Be beheaded himself by the guards before he could succeed—no. There was no vengeance in that.

It took all of Methos's will, all his experience in seeing the world's horrors, to force his face back into a cold mask. Better, far better, to live to see Nebet avenged through the destruction of king and prince and their entire world.

"A little hasty," Apophis commented dryly. "But then, a man may be excused his anger when a woman has betrayed him. No, brother," he added to the grumbling Khyan, "do not fret. We shall find you another prisoner to slay for the great god Set."

In another moment, Methos knew, even his most fiercely held self-control was going to snap. He let the sword drop, not daring to note how the blade was stained with Nebet's blood. "If I may be excused?"

Fortunately for Apophis and Methos both, he was waved away without another glance.

You will die, Apophis, you and Khyan. And even your way of life shall be erased from history. I so swear it.

That night Methos spent alone and in utter, silent anguish, trying not to think of what he'd done, trying not to remember all the other losses of a long, long life, trying to believe with all his heart that Nebet had passed the Egyptian trials of the soul, had been greeted by Osiris and the other kindly gods and been welcomed into that paradise that was just like the Egypt of the living, but without the pain, the scars, the grief . . .

Oh, Nebet, Nebet . . .

Hands over his face, he abandoned himself to utter pain.

But after an eternity of night, the morning finally came, and with it new determination. Methos, weary and aching, eyes burning from lack of sleep, set out for one last royal audience. There was nothing more to be gained here. Save, if he stayed among these folk whom he had come to truly hate, his death.

King Apophis was waiting for him, looking so cruelly complacent that Methos nearly broke and blindly attacked there and then. But he would not give this cold-eyed monster the pleasure of his death.

"King Apophis, I have greatly enjoyed your hospitality in these last few weeks." Amazing how urbane, how utterly removed from emotion, his voice sounded. "But now I feel I may be of greater service elsewhere."

"Ah, the woman's death did affect you." Dark humor glinted in Apophis's eyes. "Betrayal is always painful."

"It is." *And shall prove most painful to you.*

But the king was continuing, "You have, indeed, proven your worth to us. And you are much beloved by our brother. Do you truly seek to leave?"

In other words, do you, oh prince's babysitter, mean to escape your charge?

"Not to leave, but to serve!" Methos countered. "You know of my cleverness, oh king; I show no false modesty there. Have no doubts about how I feel toward Prince Khyan," he added with careful wording. "But I know that you need to contact Pharaoh Kamose, create new terms with him."

"My courtiers," Apophis murmured, "speak a bit too freely."

"Your Majesty, I have been at your court. I have eyes, ears. And I can add this fact and that fact together and make two: You know that Kamose is young, hotheaded, and ambitious, and you therefore must make him see you are his overlord before he grows too sure of his power."

The king neither agreed nor denied. "And what has this to do with you?"

"Why, have you not already seen me debating at your court? Have you not already heard examples of my wisdom? Do you not already know I can be trusted?"

"As long as it suits you."

"No argument there, Your Majesty," Methos interjected smoothly. "But as long as you rule, you who wield the greatest power, it suits me to be trustworthy to you!"

Daringly, he grinned, and saw the king's grudging grin in return. Pressing the advantage, Methos continued, "And is not a trusted, clever ambassador of greater worth to a king than a mere . . . companion?"

Apophis, like the politician all kings must be, dipped his head in reluctant agreement. "True enough."

"And have you, in all honesty, a more clever ambassador than I? One who knows more about Kamose and his brother?"

"One who knows more about the lack of such ambassadors within my own court," the king added dryly. "Very well, then. It will be you who takes my message to Pharaoh Kamose and informs him of the new concessions he must make as our loyal vassal."

"And if he kills the messenger of that ill news, why, then you have all the more reason to destroy him. Understood."

"Clever, indeed," the king said with a wry twist of a smile. "Ah, but the desert and river are filled with perils! An armed escort will accompany you, of course."

"Of course."

"As," Apophis added with a thin smile, "will my brother himself."

Not taking any chances of my getting away, are we? "As Your Majesty wills it," Methos said smoothly. "Prince Khyan and I shall go to Thebes together, and return with a message of utter submission."

Yours, that is. And may your submission, oh you slayer of the innocent, be most painful, lingering, and filled with despair.

Chapter Nineteen

Egypt, the Banks of the Nile: 1573 B.C.

They sailed out of Avaris on the next morning's tide, Methos and Khyan and the promised armed escort. Methos, still worn and weary with stifled grief, leaned on the rail for a last look at the fortress, saying a final silent farewell to Nebet.

And a threat to the Hyksos.

The next time I see you, oh Avaris, it will be as your destroyer.

Khyan, fortunately, was in one of his silent periods, brooding like a child, seeing who knew what visions. If he had babbled or, worse, so much as mentioned Nebet, Methos knew he would not have been able to stop himself from blindly attacking.

But whichever gods there might be not only kept Khyan still, they had also sent a strong wind to the south, carrying the ship swiftly up the Nile. Soon the Hyksos capital was out of sight. Methos straightened, feeling a psychic weight lifting from his spirit at the sight of free, vast, near-eternal Egypt under the clear blue desert sky, at the Nile flowing past open land and plain, ordinary villages as it had for more millennia than any but an Immortal could understand.

And he gladly shifted his thoughts from Avaris and the darkness within that place to the relative sunlight of the Egyptian court at Thebes—and to what by now must be the beginnings of a true army. Yes, and to what would still need to be done on that account. . . .

He and the royal Egyptian brothers had already agreed that they would need horses. But he'd told them that judicious thefts and a wait of three years or so would ensure the literal birth of a cavalry force. He would be able to help out with that; he had experience with horses where the Egyptians did not. And, of course, the Egyptians would also be needing schooling in the handling of war chariots.

No, wait. Methos's grip tightened on the ship's rail. Interesting thought . . . yes . . .

Yes, indeed. If his plan was correct, they would not need to depend on chariots or horses very much after all, only sufficient proficiency with the new weaponry . . . the bows and swords . . . and ships.

No difficulty there. The Egyptians already had sufficient ships to launch a naval attack, yes, and to carry adequate supplies to keep their army fed—fed for however long it took for them to trap the Hyksos within their own fortress, their own waterless fortress.

Methos deliberately let himself sink into all the myriad details of a military campaign. They left no room for other thoughts.

Save for one: getting away from his unwanted escorts.

There were horses on board. Once they put ashore for the night, Methos decided, he would be able to steal one of them, and, assuming that the beast had been broken to riding as well as chariot-pulling, escape cross-country, straight to Thebes.

But as the day sank into night, Captain Intef, a solid man of middle years and miscellaneous ancestry, showed no signs of putting in to shore.

Of course not, Methos realized. *That cursed wind is still as strong as before. The captain's not about to waste it.*

He endured. Endured Khyan's overenthusiastic friendship, endured the prince's just as overenthusiastic gloating over cruelties performed or yet to be performed. And through it all, he clung fervently to one thought: Nebet was free.

Am I becoming a religious man? Methos wondered wryly at that. *Well, maybe, maybe not. Time enough for philosophy later. But if there is Anyone or Ones listening, let that One or Ones know that I pray that Nebet has found her own joyous immortality.*

With that, having no other means of escaping his unwanted companions, Methos settled down on deck to sleep. Or at least to as deep a sleep as he could manage with another—and potentially dangerous—Immortal on board. That meant, naturally, almost no genuine slumber and little true rest, but, he thought, one took what one was given.

This included being wakened at an unearthly hour, just when he actually had succeeded in sliding into a brief patch of sleep, by one of Khyan's usual nightmares. *This time,* Methos thought from where he lay, *I will not comfort him. This time, let him suffer.*

Waiting for the prince's shouts to settle to whimpers and then into silence, he toyed with the idea of slipping overboard then and there and swimming to shore, then finding a fishing boat. But the sudden glint of moonlight on what was assuredly not a log put an end to that thought.

I can't risk having Khyan reach Thebes before me to spread tales about King Apophis's new advisor.

At last daylight came, and with it, to Methos's great relief, the gradual diminishing of the wind.

"Oars out!" Captain Intef ordered, and the sailors began to row their determined way on up the Nile.

Now let them only put ashore for the night!

But once again, they did not. Instead, for whatever wary reason, Captain Intef had their ship anchored in the middle of the Nile.

"Is that wise?" Methos asked him in apparent innocent curiosity. "Might another ship run into us in the darkness?"

That earned him a mildly contemptuous glance. "No one will be sailing at night!"

"Except for the occasional smuggler?" Methos suggested.

"The Hyksos regime does not permit smugglers."

"Ah, forgive me, Captain Intef. I had forgotten the strength of the Hyksos rule."

Indeed I had not forgotten. That which is too strong to bend can, instead, be broken.

Methos set about working on Khyan instead, reminding the prince of how wonderful roasted duck could be, painting a delectable word picture of a duck turning on a spit, basted with its own juices, the steam rising into the night air, so wonderfully savory. . . .

"Yes!" the prince exclaimed. "We shall have roasted duck this night!"

"But Prince Khyan," Captain Intef began warily, "we dare not risk open flame aboard ship."

Methos waited, anticipating . . . yes!

"Then put ashore!" came the autocratic command.

"But the men— the horses—it will take so long to get all unloaded and then reloaded in the morning."

"Do you question me? Do you dare?"

"No, Prince Khyan," the captain said in resignation. "Never."

As Intef began shouting orders to his men, Khyan turned to Methos in triumph. "You see, Methos? You see how they dare not disobey me? This night we shall have a hot, fresh meal!"

Methos nodded and smiled. *This night I shall escape from the lot of you!*

But it wasn't as easy to slip away into the darkness as Methos had expected. The guards weren't the problem: Well fed and groggy from their meal, they were definitely less than alert, drifting off to sleep one by lazy one. After all, why bother to keep a stern watch? No one was likely to be about this region save for the occasional farmer, and what had such as they to fear from a farmer?

Khyan was another matter, alert and aware of every shadow, clinging to Methos like a child.

"Nothing is lurking out there," Methos tried to assure him. "Nothing but—"

"There! Look, there! Eyes!"

"That? That is nothing but a tiny, tiny jackal trying to steal scraps of food from our camp."

"That is Anubis! Anubis the jackal god is watching us!"

Methos gave up trying to explain. "You should not fear him! Are you not protected by a greater god?"

"Set!" Khyan exclaimed. "Set will protect me!"

Unfortunately, Set isn't going to silence him, Methos thought. Instead, as though newly inspired, the prince followed him about wherever Methos tried to settle down, insisting on telling story after story, sharing confidence after confidence.

And none of it making any sense. Damn you, man, will you never be still?

But even Khyan had to sleep *sometime,* so Methos bided his time.

And bided it some more.

At last, pushing the issue a bit, he feigned a yawn, then another. "Forgive me," Methos told the prince, "but I really must sleep a bit."

"Ah, of course. You are not as strong as one protected by Set. By all means, sleep."

"Even you, oh prince, really should take some rest. You do not want to show Set you think so little of the gift of life."

"Oh. Never. Good idea. Good idea."

Methos lay still, waiting . . . not yet . . . Khyan was still stirring restlessly, murmuring something about "Set . . . nothing to fear . . ."

Ah, silence at last. Utter, utter silence, save for the occasional stamp of a horse's hoof and the chirring of insects. Methos slowly, warily sat up, looking around. Someone had banked the campfire, and he waited for his eyes to fully adjust to the darkness.

Yes. All of them were asleep.

I could kill them one by one—no. Not all of them deserve to be murdered in their sleep.

Let them die on the battlefield instead? Was that really a better death?

Philosophy at some other time, Methos chided himself. The hard fact of it was that no matter how wary, no one man could slay so many others without making *some* noise, waking someone and getting himself killed.

Warily, he got to his feet, holding his breath, then crept step by silent step toward the horses, praying that none of them would whinny. He reached out a slow hand to the nearest, letting the animal catch his scent, lip his hand, even swipe a wet pink tongue across his palm for the salt.

"Good, very good," he murmured to the horse.

Carefully, Methos slipped a makeshift rope bridle over the horse's head, then stepped softly away, looking about for tack. He could, if he must, ride bareback, but it would be so much easier if only he could find—

A heavy body tackled him, sending him crashing down, fortunately into noise-muffling sand. Methos twisted frantically about—

Khyan!

"Traitor!" the prince hissed. "Demon!"

Methos struck, fist catching Khyan in the throat. As the prince fell backward, choking, but still clinging to him, Methos struggled to draw his sword. But there wasn't room in these close quarters, and Khyan, already recovered, was trying to draw his blade as well. Methos lunged at him again, and the two Immortals went sprawling, struggling with each other, both trying to get their weapons free—Methos trying above all to keep the fight *quiet!*

He's strong, too strong, can't hold him—ha, wait!

He closed a hand on the hilt of Khyan's dagger, thought, *Yes,* twisted it free, and stabbed with all his might, up under Khyan's ribs, stabbed again and again, choking the prince on his own blood so he wouldn't cry out with his dying breath.

Yes! Khyan was, for however short a while, dead.

Can't risk taking his head, damn him, not when a Quickening would draw the guards. Some other time, Khyan, I promise.

Never mind wasting more time hunting for a saddle. Methos hurled himself onto the horse he'd befriended, only to nearly get himself thrown as the animal shied in terror from the reek of fresh blood. But he clung to the slick back and short-cut mane with the strength of desperation. And fortunately this horse seemed to have been broken to riding, because it didn't try to buck him off more than once.

With a slap on the neck and a kick with both heels, Methos urged his mount forward, and the horse gladly burst into a full, frenzied gallop, eager to outrun the smell of blood. Bending low over the tossing mane, feeling the powerful equine muscles bunching and releasing under him and hearing the wind rushing by his ears, Methos could have laughed his satisfaction. But not yet, not till they'd traveled long enough to open up a good lead. Long enough to make pursuit away from the ship impractical— particularly since the Hyksos would be caught up in a storm of confusion about their blood-covered yet miraculously unharmed prince. And if he cut directly overland, he would reach Thebes just ahead of the ship, which must follow the curve of the Nile.

To Thebes! Methos thought and dared not shout. *To Thebes—and vengeance!*

Chapter Twenty

Ironic, Duncan MacLeod thought, terribly ironic that a killer should be hunting here: Riverside Park was one of the lovelier, more peaceful stretches of greenery in Manhattan. A long, narrow, cleverly landscaped park placed so that nothing seemed to come between a visitor and a fine view of the Hudson River, it also muffled as much of the city noise as was possible.

Oh, yes, and so whatever happens here at night is also muffled from the city, thought MacLeod. *Ideal for lovers. And predators.*

MacLeod and Methos had just come across the latest site of the West Side Slayer's attack, an area roped off by the inevitable yellow tape reading, POLICE LINE. DO NOT CROSS. There was little to see now, save for a few busy police officials, police photographers going over every inch of ground, and what were presumably police lab technicians taking soil samples. Nothing, MacLeod thought, to show that two young people had died here last night.

He glanced around. A news van, station logo plastered on the side, was parked up on Riverside Drive, the reporters inside presumably hoping for one more gory bit of news. And a group of tourists, recognizable as such by their barrage of cameras, were watching the police proceedings as though this were just another form of entertainment.

Entertainment!

"Tourists will be tourists," Methos murmured. "Should have seen them in old Rome, rooting for the lions."

MacLeod glanced sharply at him. "There are two kids dead here. And there are going to be more dead kids if we can't find the killer. I take it there's nothing you can use?"

"No. The place has been too thoroughly trampled. MacLeod, just because I don't wail and tear my clothes in grief doesn't mean I don't feel *something*. Mostly," he added, "frustration."

"Frustration," MacLeod echoed without expression. "Come on, let's go look at the river."

Without another word, he started south, and after a second, Methos followed.

New Yorkers, though, were a hardy lot. Since everyone knew that the West Side Slayer struck only at night, and it was now early afternoon, life went on. As they left the murder scene behind them, MacLeod and Methos passed a few locals who seemed utterly unworried about crime: a young woman dog-walking her half-dozen charges on their leashes, who gave both Immortals an appreciative grin in passing; a scruffy teenage boy engrossed in pinning up flyers on every lamppost, fence, and even the occasional tree (was there really, MacLeod wondered, a band called Elektrik Kows?); and one bedraggled homeless man lost in a happy world of his own.

Only the patrolling policemen and -women looked grim, glances missing nothing. MacLeod knew that he and Methos had been instantly summed up by them as "businessmen, out-of-towners, no problem."

True enough. For them, at any rate.

To his left was the busy, modern flow of traffic on the West Side Highway, though the clever landscaping almost hid it from sight, and up on the drive, the elegant townhouses MacLeod recalled from Edmund Branson's time, now mostly subdivided into high-priced apartments. To the right stretched the width of the equally busy Hudson River, filled just now with a freighter, a good-sized sloop headed, presumably, for the Seventy-ninth Street Boat Basin, and some daring soul in what looked like a one-man kayak.

He stifled an impatient sigh. "Not much like the Nile."

Methos raised a shoulder in an absent-minded shrug. "Not all that different: That was a commercial river, too. Lots of boat traffic up and down it every day. Unless," he added wryly, "I'm getting my memories mixed up with some *National Geographic Special.*"

But then he stopped to look out over the river, his face unreadable, his eyes grown shadowed once more. "Must be frustrating the hell out of Khyan, too," Methos added, so softly that MacLeod almost didn't hear him.

"Just how far back do you two go?"

"Far enough."

"Damn it, Methos, this 'everything's a secret' routine is getting to be a pain. All right, admit this much: You two are old enemies."

" 'Old' is the operative word for it, yes." Methos never so much as glanced MacLeod's way. "I thought he was dead, I truly did." A long pause. "I did kill him once."

Then Methos shrugged and turned away from the river, starting forward again. "Unfortunately, as I said, I didn't get the chance to finish the job, take his head. So it goes."

"You seem amazingly calm about it!"

"Not calm," Methos corrected. "Merely accepting."

"But—"

"Look, I'm not denying that once upon a time I would have taken his head with a great deal of joy, and maybe even have done a good deal worse to him first. But that was a long time ago, in a very different world. A man changes."

He fell silent, walking on as though MacLeod weren't even there. But MacLeod couldn't let it drop just like that. "I'd like to have *some* idea of what we're up against! You do still hate him, don't you?"

"Do I?" But then Methos's sly smile faded, and he gave the smallest of reluctant sighs. "Don't you see, Duncan?

It's just been too damned long. The fire dims with the centuries, the hate, the rage, the . . . grief. Given enough time, you come to see just how small one person really is. The world, the universe, is all just too vast for that one small person to make any major changes."

"Are you saying we should do nothing?" MacLeod asked indignantly. "Just—sit back and let evil flourish?"

"Save me from melodramatic Celts!" Ignoring MacLeod's wryly raised eyebrow, Methos continued, "No, my wild Highlander, I am not saying that at all, merely that one man, even one Immortal working with all the goodwill in the world, can't cram all evil into a neat little package and remodel . . . it."

"What is it?"

Methos stopped short, staring at him. "Well, isn't memory an amazing thing? Remodeling that neat little package, indeed—I've just remembered something nasty about Hyksos beliefs. The something I almost recalled back in the coffee shop."

"Something nasty in the sense of useful to us, I take it?"

"Ohhh yes. You see, the Hyksos believed that a soul captured in an artifact could still be tormented by anyone with sufficient arcane skill."

"Which you have?" MacLeod asked wryly.

"Which I can fake. Listen." Quickly, Methos summarized his idea, concluding. "If we can get our hands on the Hyksos sword, we can almost certainly lure Khyan right to us."

"Ah, you do realize what you're saying, don't you? We can hardly call up Professor Maxwell and ask, 'Can we borrow an item from your exhibit?' "

Methos only shrugged.

MacLeod gave a sharp little laugh. "Oh, right. After five thousand years or so, a little art theft hardly seems memorable."

"Something like that. We've both garnered enough, shall we say, professional experience in that area, so . . ."

"If Amanda learns about this, she will never, ever let me hear the end of it."

"That, my dear MacLeod, is your problem."

He had been wandering aimlessly since morning, down by the huge bulk of the docked USS *Intrepid,* his mind seeing not the modern warship museum with its berthed but still deadly looking warplanes, but casting up images of an earlier world, another river. . . .

Yes, he could almost see the *right* boats now, the *proper* boats, with their rectangular sails, their curving prows and sterns . . . it was then, then, and his brother was still alive and he was happy at his brother's side, safe, loved—

But the harsh *blaaat* of an impudent ferry cut into the image, shattering it back into sharp reality, and for a moment he could almost have wept over the shock and disappointment.

"I will find you," he vowed, "find you, yes, find you and free you."

A passing sailor gave him a startled glance at that and said to his fellow, touching his head, *"C'est un fou!"*

This is a crazy man. French. He knew that much French, picked up somewhere, somewhen in his wanderings. *A crazy man.*

And the other sailor was laughing and agreeing, *"Un fou, vraiment!"*

Truly a crazy man! For one wild instant, he almost drew his sword to avenge the insult—

No. Not by day. Too many witnesses would bring those officers of the law. He could not afford to have his mission, his sacred, desperate mission, interrupted.

A crazy man.

Was he that? Was he insane? *Brother, brother, help me! I am lost and alone—help me!*

But of course there was no answer. "I am not crazy," he snapped at the sailors. "Oh you of no worth at all, I am of royal blood!"

Ignoring their startled stares, he hurried on his way,

shivering, heading blindly north. Start with the young, start with the young, kill and kill each night for as long as it took, till this land was a desert . . .

More children, he thought.

He would kill more children.

Here I sit on a park bench, MacLeod thought, *like someone out of a bad caper movie, plotting to rob a museum. Yes, and I've got a man next to me who remembers when the artifacts in there were all new.*

Just another day in New York City.

". . . and so," he continued, "we should be able to bypass the alarms that Maxwell so kindly told me about. Once we're on that balcony, there shouldn't be any real difficulty for one of us to climb down the—"

Both Immortals came starkly alert, glancing swiftly about, MacLeod on his feet, hand near the hilt of his sword.

But in the next moment, that sharp warning of a nearby Immortal had gone, leaving the two of them staring at each other. MacLeod did a quick prowl of the area, but saw and felt nothing unlikely. At last, reluctantly, he gave up the hunt and returned to the bench, where Methos was sitting like a statue named "Tension."

"Nothing, I take it," Methos said.

"Nothing." As MacLeod sat back down, he suggested, "In a city this size, there are certainly going to be other Immortals." Come to think of it, he had already come across two in separate incidents, one a harried-looking businessman not at all interested in meeting him, the other a young woman who'd given him one worried glance and hastily disappeared onto a subway train. "It . . . could have been another one of us," MacLeod continued, "some totally innocent soul with no intention of getting involved in the Game today."

"It could," Methos agreed.

A pause. Then MacLeod continued, "And neither of us is buying that for a moment."

"No." Methos stretched out his legs, crossing them in deceptive laziness at the ankle. "Our brief visitor could only have been Khyan, although he didn't stay around long enough for any positive ID. I doubt that we've frightened him off for good, though."

The teen who'd been plastering up the notices about Elektrik Kows, working his way south, had been watching the sudden flurry of action with great interest. At MacLeod's cold stare, the boy shrugged as if to say, "It's cool," and returned to his papering job.

"Besides," Methos continued, indicating the teen with a dip of the head, "we can hardly get into any, shall we say, encounters here and now, not with inconvenient witnesses likely to stop by and watch the show. Not that it matters, though, since what we actually need is to lure Khyan away from here."

"Precisely. And," MacLeod added, glancing thoughtfully at the busy teen again, "I think I know how we can do it."

He stood in the shadow of a monument somewhere farther north in the park, without any knowledge of which it was or how he'd gotten here.

The shock of it! The sudden awareness of That Other, the one whose name . . . he had forgotten the name just now. But it didn't matter. That had been *he,* That One who had also been touched by a god . . . not Set, but some enemy deity who clearly still watched over him—yes. How else could That Other have survived and have come here, *here* of all places—

The sword! That Other, too, must seek the sword!

He will not have it. I shall stop him, slay him, cut off his head, and carve out his entrails. He stiffened as though stabbed through the heart. *That is it!*

The full glory of realization tore through him, making him throw back his head and laugh with wild joy, heedless of the small minds who gawked at him.

That is what Set wishes me to do! That is why he brought

*me here! Tonight, yes, yes, I shall find That Other some-
where here—*
  Tonight shall I kill him!

"First," MacLeod said, "to set the trap."

He'd led Methos to one of the many copy stores to be
found all over the city, this one, conveniently enough, lo-
cated right on Seventy-second Street. Methos stood at a
counter, staring at a blank sheet of paper, chewing absently
on the end of the marker.

*As though he held a quill pen, or maybe even an older
world's stylus,* MacLeod mused, and, at the thought of
Methos, clay tablets, and a morass of ancient memories
asked, "Hello? Are you still here?"

That got him a sharp sideways glare. "What do you expect? I haven't used the language in almost three thousand
years! It's not easy to remember . . . not that a madman's in
any condition to care if my grammar's correct, but I have
to get the message clear enough for him to read. . . . Yes."

With that, Methos bent over the page, slowly and carefully drawing the message in what looked to MacLeod like
rather shakily drawn Egyptian hieroglyphs. "There. I *think*
that's right. Now . . ."

He added a second message in what MacLeod had to assume was equally shaky but reasonably accurate Hyksos.

"That should do it. Ah, yes, miss. I'm ready. We'd
like . . . oh, I'd say five hundred copies of this ought to do
the job. Right?" he added to MacLeod.

"Right." *If we can't do the job with five hundred, then
five thousand wouldn't make a difference.*

Five hundred copies run off on a high-speed copier took
very little time. As MacLeod paid the young woman,
Methos took the package with a wry, "The wonders of
modern technology."

Back they went to Riverside Park, armed with a staple
gun and several rolls of tape. What followed was an intensive two-man papering campaign, putting up the makeshift
posters all over the park area.

"Most of those," MacLeod said, seeing how many of the Elektrik Kows signs had already vanished, "are going to disappear in a short time, torn down by vandals or maybe just the wind. But with any luck, enough will remain just long enough."

"And if they do," Methos added, "*and* if Khyan returns to this area . . ."

"We've baited our trap with something only he can read!"

For the hieroglyphs, Egyptian and Hyksos both, said point-blank:

"The sword in which a king's soul lies captive can be found atop the Branson Collection. There, a dark ritual will be performed this very night. There shall a king's soul be cast into eternal torment!"

Methos glanced at MacLeod, face its usual emotionless mask. "Assuming that he really is insane enough to believe that nonsense, and not so insane that he can no longer read the hieroglyphs, it's now just a matter of waiting."

"Not quite," MacLeod said. "Now we have a museum to rob!"

Chapter Twenty-one

Egypt, Thebes: Reign of Pharaoh Kamose, Circa
1573–1570 B.C.

An exhausted Methos on an exhausted horse reached
Thebes after a frantic few days of gallop, walk, trot, gallop—the varying gaits the only way to keep a horse on an
endurance run such as this from collapsing under its
rider—only to be greeted just outside the city walls by an
escort of guards armed with the new Hyksos-styled
weapons and quite startled to see someone approach from
overland.

"Yes, it's me, Methos, truly it is, not some desert
demon!" Methos snapped impatiently, his throat so dry he
could hardly get the words out. "Has Prince Khyan's ship
arrived yet? No? Excellent! I must speak with Pharaoh
Kamose or Prince Ahmose as swiftly as possible—but out
here. Yes! I said out here! The fewer folks who see me, the
safer for everyone. Hurry, damn you! Prince Khyan's ship
can't be far from Thebes."

The minutes seemed to creep by, painfully slowly, but at
last Prince Ahmose appeared, looking harried and as wary
as it was possible for so young a prince to look.

"Methos! What is this nonsense?"

"Prince Khyan will be here very shortly," Methos told
him, with only the most perfunctory of salutes, "with demands for your royal brother. Don't try to argue with him.
Don't try reason at all: The man is totally insane, utterly

unpredictable, and potentially deadly. Just agree to whatever terms the Hyksos demand and get him out of Thebes as quickly as possible."

"Lie, you mean."

Methos was too weary for patience. "Oh, you aren't going to go utterly honorable now, are you? Your nation's safety is at stake!"

Anger glinted in Ahmose's eyes at the brusque tone. "What about you?"

"I'll be hiding out in the desert." *Beyond the range of an Immortal's senses.* "Prince Khyan and the others must not find me here, for all our sakes."

"He must also, I assume," Prince Ahmose added, "not know you're still alive."

Thank you for being so quick-witted! "That would make our lives far less complicated, yes. I don't suppose you could arrange . . . ?"

"Some false evidence? Oh, yes." The prince hesitated a moment, then burst out, "Of course! It's so simple. You see, my brother had a murderer executed just yesterday. And while the criminal didn't look very much like you, a severed head that has been rather . . . chewed up by the desert vermin won't be so easily identifiable." The prince smiled thinly. "I think we can safely offer up a dead 'Methos' to King Apophis!"

"Prince Ahmose, I salute you, one survivor to another. And now, so that I may go right on surviving . . ."

"Ah, yes. You, and you, go with him," he ordered the nearby guards. "The Red Cliff Oasis. That," he added to Methos, "should be far and obscure enough for safety, and you shall find enough there to keep you entertained while waiting. We shall talk after the Hyksos prince is gone."

"We shall, indeed. Till later, Prince Ahmose!"

To Methos's fierce delight, the Red Cliff Oasis—which lived up to its name by being a desert plain touched with green from a spring and ringed round by stark red cliffs—turned out to be a secret military training ground. Nodding approval, he watched men practicing with newly forged Hyksos-design swords and axes and powerful compound bows, most of them wearing Egyptian improvisations of the Hyksos bronze scale tunics. These newly fledged warriors were still a good way from being an organized, efficient military force, but in the short time since he'd been gone, they had come a long way, indeed.

Patriotism is a marvelous motivating factor. And—oh, Apophis, but you are in for a very nasty surprise!

Methos, armed with a wider knowledge of warfare than was possible for these relatively nonmilitaristic folk, went among the new warriors, helping this man with an improved grip on an ax, showing that man how to handle the extra pull a compound bow demanded. He worked himself as fiercely as any of the Egyptians, and welcomed the work. Military training was as useful to an Immortal as to a mortal.

Besides, his state of almost constant exhaustion left no room for . . . memories.

"You were right," Pharaoh Kamose snapped.

Late that night, word had come to the Red Cliff Oasis that it was finally safe for Methos to return to Thebes. This morning, he sat with the royal brothers about a pretty little blue-tiled table set with an ewer and cups containing cool drinks, there in the shady courtyard garden of the water lilies.

No skulls in these *trees,* Methos thought gratefully, and asked, "Your Majesty?"

"Prince Khyan *was* utterly, unbelievably insane, raving about—gods, I don't know what. That he was the chosen of Set, that he could not die—yes, that you had even tried to kill him!"

"That much," Methos said dryly, "is true. I did. Unfortunately, I failed. But King Apophis's terms . . . ?"

"Oh, we swore to them," Prince Ahmose cut in. "Swore to be good, docile, harmless vassals of our kind overlord.

And all the while," he added with a fierce grin, "our warriors continued their training out there in the desert."

"Thank you, incidentally," Kamose added, "for your assistance on that front."

"Pharaoh Kamose," Methos said in utter honesty, "I wish to see the Hyksos destroyed every bit as strongly as do you."

Kamose accepted that at face value: Why would any reasonable man not wish to see invaders repelled?

But Ahmose, being Ahmose, eyed Methos with wary speculation, wondering, no doubt, just what might have happened during that stay in Avaris.

Sorry, youngster. You may be clever, but I am very much your senior. In all things.

He met the prince's gaze levelly and gave absolutely nothing away. And after a moment, it was Ahmose who looked away, saying, "We're wasting precious time."

"We are, indeed," Methos agreed. "If you will but bring us maps, I'll show you what I've learned—and how I believe you may defeat the Hyksos."

"Maps," Kamose commanded a servant. "Now."

"'Man sent by the gods,'" Ahmose murmured without a trace of emotion, and Methos eyed him, wondering, *Jealousy? Or mere cynicism?*

"Perhaps," he said, just as neutrally. Then, in relief, "Ah, but here are the maps."

Kamose cleared a space for them with a regal sweep of a hand that sent the cups and ewer flying. "Now," he said, unrolling a map and glancing at Methos, "speak."

Methos studied the stylized designs for a moment. "We are here."

"Agreed."

"And the nearest town with ties to the Hyksos is . . ." he traced a route down the Nile, north, "here, if I'm not mistaken."

"Nefrusy," Kamose all but spat. "Yes. Nefrusy, ruled over by Teti, son of Pepi, who betrayed his own blood and turned his town into a true nest of Hyksos."

"Nefrusy," Methos commented, "with no real walls, no real fortifications."

"Yes," Ahmose added thoughtfully. "And it lies so conveniently near to the oasis roads leading on to Bahariya. That," he said to Methos, "is an oasis town which is also a Hyksos communications post. Indeed," the prince added thoughtfully, "I think it's the *only* post between Nefrusy and Avaris."

"*Tsk,*" Methos said, "The Hyksos have grown careless."

"Haven't they? We should be able to do something with that fact."

Methos grinned at him, "We should, indeed. Particularly if," he added, tracing the route on the map with a fingertip, "while Bahariya is attacked by land, the royal fleet is also headed on down the Nile to retake Memphis."

"Possible," Kamose snapped. "Probable, in fact."

"And as the fleet sails," Methos added, "it will be gathering supplies and, one assumes, volunteers along the way—and then continue on to Avaris."

"Avaris," Kamose cut in, "which, thanks to that lax Hyksos communications system, will not have advance word of our coming!"

"Or at least not credible word."

"You have a plan worked out," Ahmose said to Methos, almost accusingly.

"Assuming that your royal court agrees with this—"

"They will obey me." Kamose's voice was flat. "That is not a choice."

"I thought not. Now here," Methos continued, pointing to the map, "is what I propose. . . ."

The hour was very late when the three had completed their plotting to their mutual satisfaction, and Methos was very glad to be headed back to his room and his first night's sleep in a bed in quite some time.

He froze in the doorway at the sight of a graceful, dimly seen figure, his heart crying for an anguished instant,

Nebet! even as his mind knew that it was impossible. "Tiaa."

She stepped out of the shadows, smiling, her lovely body bare of all ornament save a single jeweled strand about her hips. "I missed you." Her voice was charmingly throaty. "I missed our little games so very, very much. But I just might forgive you for leaving, if you brought me back something pretty. Have you brought me anything?"

"Isn't it enough that I brought myself back?"

She pouted deliciously. "Of course, but . . . I would have liked a little something. Just a trinket to show that you cared. . . . You do care, don't you?"

She was lovely, desirable, there for the taking. And Methos felt nothing but despair.

Too soon. It is far too soon after Nebet's death.

"Forgive me, Tiaa," he said. "This night I am too weary for more than sleep. Alone."

Her eyes widened with disbelief. "Oh," she said after a moment. "Well. So be it. There are others who will more properly appreciate what you reject."

With an insulted switch of her rounded hips, Tiaa snatched up her pleated linen robe and left.

Lovely. But so very shallow. "Have you brought me anything?" Nebet would never have . . .

No. He would not brood on what was and was no more. And he really was every bit as weary as he'd told Tiaa. Methos fell into bed and, mercifully, did not dream.

He woke to a summons from Dowager Queen Teti-sheri. Freshly dressed and groomed, Methos found her sitting quite regally in her garden, her handmaidens, pretty young things in flowing linen and strings of glittering beads, chattering like so many chirping birds, gathered around her.

"Leave us," the queen said to them, not unkindly. "Do stop fussing, Bebi! Leave us. I will not harm this young man's honor."

In a flurry of giggles and sly glances at Methos, the girls scurried off.

"Silly things," Teti-sheri said fondly. "I never did bear a *gentle* daughter, just Ahhotep, fierce as her late husband and showing more of our Minoan ancestry than do I. Though she did give me two lovely grandsons. And I do admit that she is more sensible than her husband, my hot-headed stepson I never could quite love."

Sensible, indeed: Methos knew that what Ahhotep was doing in southern Egypt wasn't merely tending estates: She was as good as any war leader holding the south safe for her sons.

And in the process, avoiding conflict with her equally strong-willed mother. She probably finds it easier to fight with the Nubians!

"Though I did love his father," the queen continued, "he who is now a god among gods and, no doubt, still quarreling with his son."

She looked up at Methos with, he thought, the studied innocence of a cat asking, *What* cream? "Do I shock you, Methos?"

He bowed. "Your Majesty, nothing you could say could shock me."

"Such a gallant liar. I knew you would return," she added sedately. "Did I not tell you that you would be protected?"

At his involuntary flinch, his thought of Nebet, who had not been protected, the queen nodded, her eyes suddenly very gentle. "Why do you think I hesitated when you asked if you would return safely from Avaris?"

"There is other than physical harm."

"My dear, do you think I don't know that? I, who have lost a husband, a stepson, and all too soon will lose a grandson as well?"

Oh, these fragile, fragile mortals!

But fragility was just not the word to apply to Teti-sheri. Looking deeply into his eyes with her wise, ancient gaze, she said, as calmly as though commenting on the weather, "Of course you miss her. But she is safe."

Guessing at the true reason for his grief? Or speaking

through the forced honesty of her Gift? Methos knew he would get no answer if he asked. And he did not wish to ask.

"Thank you," he murmured. "I—"

"Walk warily," she cut in, so suddenly that Methos nearly started. Her eyes wide and visionary, the queen told him, "You shall aid my grandsons, and aid them well. But . . . walk warily."

"Ah, might I ask for some specific details?"

"No. I fear not. The vision has gone. But you have already walked warily for many years, haven't you? So now. Continue to do so.

"Now, off with you. I wish to be alone."

Methos stood with Kamose and Ahmose, looking out over the Red Cliff Oasis to where the warriors trained.

"*Now* they look ready!" the pharaoh boasted with an expansive gesture over the practice field. "*Now* they look like an army."

Methos had to admit that they were much improved, bowmen protecting infantry, assault teams practicing with swift rushes and fierce attacks, and cavalrymen on their precious horses cutting down targets to left and right with sword and spear.

But are they going to look so deadly against living foes?

At least these weren't all amateurs, not anymore. Methos and Ahmose had persuaded the pharaoh to hire a troop of mercenaries as well, the Medjai, deadly archers from the deserts on the eastern side of the Nile, fierce, dark-skinned, proud men (though not too proud to take a pharaoh's gold) who hated the Hyksos—as, indeed, they would have hated any other invaders. Interspaced with the Egyptians, they gave Kamose's young army some much-needed military experience.

"Hear me, oh my troops!" Kamose shouted, his voice echoing off the cliffs. "The time has come! No longer will we need bend our knee to the Hyksos might. Now shall we sweep down the Nile like a blast of fire! Now shall We, your pharaoh, fight with the false one who names himself Apophis, now shall We rend him apart!

"Now shall Egypt be delivered from the Hyksos yoke!

"Now shall Egypt once again be free!"

Chapter Twenty-two

Egypt, the Nile and Avaris: Reigns of Pharaoh Kamose and King Apophis, 1570 B.C.

Kill and kill again, think of nothing but Nebet, this is for you, Nebet, I avenge you again and yet again—

Methos, red-dripping sword in hand, wheeled his horse about, looking this way and that, hunting more foes, the wildness of battle blazing through him. All about him, the city of Nefrusy, treacherous Nefrusy that had dared to bow down to the Hyksos, lay in flaming ruins, smoke billowing up to darken the sky. The Hyksos garrison had been caught utterly, fatally, off its guard, and now its leader lay dead, the traitor Teti dead at his side, its soldiers and Nefrusy's common folk cut down alike by the Egyptian army—harvested like the wheat, Methos thought wildly, before the reaper.

And I am a reaper. I am a blade to take their lives—

No. No, calm. Wariness. Too easy for someone lurking in the ruins to throw a knife, fell him, behead him before he could recover. He stood panting, glancing about, struggling for breath and composure amid the chaos of screams and smoke and crackling flames.

Ah, but here came Kamose, proud and tall in his war chariot, sword as red as Methos's own, eyes as fierce, and all Methos could think at the sight was, *Fool, fool of a leader, to so expose yourself to danger!*

"Sire, get back to the ships!" he shouted. "There is nothing more for you here."

"The first blow!" Kamose shouted back at him. "The first blow struck, the first step taken on the path to victory!"

No place for niceties. "There will be no second step if you do not get yourself to safety!"

He wasted no time insisting the pharaoh listen to reason, or seeing if Kamose had actually heeded him. Instead, Methos, reminding himself that he had work yet to be done, set about rounding up the men in his own division, those who had proven themselves skilled enough in the new art of horsemanship to risk the Egyptian force's precious few mounts.

"Leave the looting!" he shouted at them. "Leave it!" He slapped one man, hard, with the flat of his sword, leaving a bloody mark across the man's arm. "There will be richer loot when Avaris is taken. But now we must ride! Do you hear me? Apophis must not learn of this attack!"

That forced some ragged cheers from them. Weary though they must surely be by now, they leaped onto their horses with at least an attempt at grace. Methos in their lead, they rode out of the charred ruins of Nefrusy, on out over the desert, still fierce as flame, northwest toward the oasis town of Bahariya and the crucial road overland to Avaris.

No great force at Bahariya, if the royal spies were right. They'd best be right; I hardly have the men to take it else.

An agreeable surprise waited there, though: Bahariya, a small cluster of mud brick houses around the central water, surrendered gleefully to the pharaoh's suddenly arrived representatives without even a token struggle, greeting Methos and his men with Hyksos bodies laid out by local knives and cries of, "Freedom! Long live the pharaoh!"

They had no idea which pharaoh it might be, nor did they much care. These desert folk were not Egyptians, but they far preferred the freedom they'd had under Egyptian rule to the dictates of the Hyksos. Kamose it was these days? Good enough! Someone snatched up a flute, someone else a drum, and dancing sprang into being so suddenly that the horses shied.

"Come, warriors, dance with us! Water your horses, then yourselves!"

It was palm wine being flourished in those earthen jugs.

Yes, and sleep with our daughters, Methos thought, *and bring some brave new blood into the tribe. I know how this type of celebration ends up. Not that they'll sire any babies from me.*

But even as his warriors and the desert people were congratulating each other, the desert women already eyeing the warriors, and in particular Methos, with speculative glances, Methos saw one man steal away from the others, heading for the Hyksos messengers' stable. Following, Methos saw him leap onto a horse with the ease of long familiarity.

No, you don't!

He sprang back onto his own horse despite its protests, urging it forward. At the sound of pursuing hoofbeats, the Hyksos messenger turned in the saddle, face wild with sudden alarm.

Yes, fear me, fear your death!

The Hyksos rode now at a full gallop, bent low over his horse's neck, but Methos rode his mount just as well, remembering breakneck gallops over the Asiatic steppes in the company of nomads as savage as their ponies. Methos felt his lips draw back from his teeth in a feral grin, and his sword glinted in his steady hand. He was gaining on the prey, gaining . . .

Yes! A ferocious sideways slash took the man's head, sent the messenger's body tumbling to the ground. The messenger's horse galloped on in terror, but Methos, fighting his own frantic horse, brought the animal to a sliding, trembling stop.

He was trembling now himself. Easy enough to understand that reaction to the battle and to this last bit of violence was at last hitting home. Not so easy to block out memories: the sword dripping red, the dying men staring at him, the screams and the stench . . .

There was no one to see this understandable but still demeaning loss of self-control, fortunately. Of course, Methos told himself, even if someone had seen, there was no true shame to it. Every warrior suffered some reaction sooner or later, some realization that those bodies he'd cut down had held life just a short while before, some realization that it might have been him lying dead on the field instead of them.

But Methos thought with a renewed shudder that in his case there had been more to it. Gods, yes. It had been so simple to kill and kill and kill, here, back in Nefrusy, so simple and so . . . enjoyable. Had those he'd slain been all warriors? Had there, instead, been women, children, among them? He didn't think so, but he couldn't be quite sure; he couldn't quite remember all the details of that savage, joyous madness.

Someone was coming—a few of his men, leaving the celebration to see where he'd gone. Methos straightened in the saddle, forcing his face back to coldness. He reached down with his sword, stabbed the papyrus roll the messenger had let fall, and glanced at the contents.

So now! Eyebrows raised, Methos gave a silent whistle as he read the hastily penned hieroglyphs. This was a far more dangerous message than anyone had expected—and it was very fortunate, indeed, that the messenger had been stopped.

But the message was not for these men's ears. Methos said only a curt, "There will be no advance message to Apophis," indicating the fallen body. "Pharaoh Kamose's ships are now as safe as we can make them."

"What now?" one of the men asked.

"Now," Methos told him dryly, "we rest our horses and ourselves. Tomorrow we ride on northeast across the land to join the pharaoh at Memphis. Then—on to Avaris."

"On to Avaris!" they echoed, as though he'd given them a war cry. "On to Avaris!"

* * *

They sped cross-country like fiery spirits in the next two days, cutting down whatever Hyksos made the mistake of trying to block their path, being cheered by Egyptians who realized the time of revolt was finally at hand. They came to the bank of the Nile on the morning of the third day, in time to rejoin Kamose's warriors in the process of retaking Memphis.

The cavalry's presence, Methos thought, wasn't really needed. As with Bahariya, this was almost a token fight: Memphis was still, even after near-destruction and a hundred years of occupation, very much an Egyptian city at its heart. The citizens swarmed into the streets, storming the estate of their Hyksos overlord, Yokanaan. Before Kamose's forces could get to the man, the crowd had already beaten to death Yokanaan, his family, even his servants, then mobbed back out into the streets, killing any other Hyksos they happened to catch, hurling bricks and stones and whatever weapons came to hand, yelling, "Death to the overlords! Freedom! Freedom for Egypt!"

Methos glanced at Kamose in alarm. Risky enough for even a pharaoh in this growing chaos! But Kamose, leaping up onto a mound of rubble, shouted with all his force, "Stop! In the name of Egypt, hear me! In the names of all the gods of Egypt, hear me!"

The mob froze.

"These are not the enemy!" Kamose continued fiercely. "Apophis is the foe! Apophis in Avaris! Apophis is all Egypt's foe! Apophis in Avaris!"

The mob froze. "Avaris!" went up the shout from a few throats, and then, "Avaris!" shouted the others. "To Avaris!"

Even if Kamose had been so foolish, he could not have possibly taken the swarm of sudden volunteers on board the already-crowded ships. Instead, Methos saw undiscouraged throngs of untrained, badly armed men hastily kiss their wives and children good-bye and set out on foot for Avaris. They might arrive far too late to help, Methos thought with a touch of dour humor, but by all the gods, they were going to be part of the great event!

I have no intention of walking.

Instead, Methos, at the pharaoh's request, took passage aboard Kamose's own ship, the coincidentally named *Rising in Memphis,* along with the pharaoh's most elite warriors, the Medjai archers, and a cadre of priest-physicians, shaven-headed men in plain linen robes and somber expressions.

The horses had been left behind in the once-again-Egyptian city: From this point on, there would be no need for cavalry.

With a curt bow, Methos handed the papyrus he'd taken from the slain messenger to Kamose. Frowning, the pharaoh scanned its contents, then glanced at him.

"You read it?"

"Of course."

Kamose snagged Ahmose by the arm. "Brother, listen to this, the sheer nerve of this: " 'I, Apophis, Son of Ra'—an arrogant title for a Hyksos!—'I, Apophis, greet my son, the king of Nubia,' and so on, and so on, claims against my father, God-King Sekenenre, against me . . . Ha, and look here! 'Come, fare north and join me'—that Set-damned bastard was planning to catch Egypt in a vise between two armies!"

"So it would seem," Prince Ahmose murmured, and for a moment his worry for their mother, Queen Ahhotep, in the south, was very plain. But then the boy grinned. "Well intercepted, my lord Methos! Very well intercepted, indeed! No matter what other surprises may await us, at least that one has been neutralized."

Methos leaned on the rail of the *Rising in Memphis,* lost in thoughts of battles past and present. "Would you look at that?" a youthful voice asked suddenly, and he nearly started. "A whole fleet of fishing boats has joined us."

"Convenient," Methos commented, and turned to see who was beside him.

Ah yes. He'd thought he'd recognized that voice. Standing looking out over the Nile at the other ships was a young warrior, fierce as a falcon, a handful or so years older than Prince Ahmose and, just to be confusing, Methos thought, also named Ahmose. The others called him Ahmose, Son of Eben, to distinguish him from the prince, or even Ahmose-the-Soldier, and for all his youth and common birth, he already did have the hard edge to him that marked a born soldier, and the honesty of a good one.

Ahmose-the-Soldier glanced sideways at Methos with a grin. "Gods willing, we'll win glory for us and freedom for the land in this campaign—and maybe collect a mound of hands at the same time."

"I'll settle for winning us our lives, thank you." The Egyptians, Methos knew, were under orders to collect a hand from each enemy slain in the forthcoming battle of Avaris so that an accurate tally could be kept; less space-consuming than collecting heads, he thought wryly. "And if you are after a collection of hands," Methos added, "and, for that matter, the Gold of Valor"—the golden medallions granted for bravery in the field—"have, ah, fun."

"And the same good wish to you, my lord," the unflappable Ahmose-the-Soldier replied, "the same good wish to you."

Save me from the eagerness of youth!

It wasn't quite as easy as it should have been to shed the memories of his role in the sacking, no, the near-destruction, of Nefrusy.

Damn it, no. I cannot feel guilt over what happens in war, no more than would that eager young warrior out to gather himself a mound of severed hands.

Besides, if he hadn't slain that messenger, they might, indeed, as Kamose put it, be caught in a vise, having to fight on two fronts at once. Instead, they were now headed into a confrontation with the Hyksos fleet. Or, with any luck, a lack of confrontation.

Ahead, the Nile split in two, the first of the many

branchings that formed the delta and ran into the sea. Apophis, since Avaris had no safe port other than the one dock, kept his ships berthed in the less-used western division of the Nile, while Avaris lay on the eastern branch— on the northeastern side of that branch, no less, farther north than the fleet.

What a stupid thing for him to do, putting all his ships in one place, and keeping them so far from his fortress. But then, there never has been a naval battle in either culture's history; they probably never even considered the possibility of one. Till now, of course.

With that, Methos went in search of the leader of the Medjai mercenaries, a tall, lean man known only as Knife, prominent of nose and cheekbones and so dark of skin that his teeth flashed dazzlingly white when he smiled.

As he smiled now, sharp as the edge of a blade, as Methos approached. " 'Man sent by the gods.' "

The Medjai had all taken to calling him that, much to Methos's discontent; he knew the title grated on Prince Ahmose's nerves. "Are you ready?"

"Oh, indeed, yes." Knife spoke the Egyptian tongue fluently, though with a clipped accent. "You have truly seen this technique done elsewhere? Successfully?"

"Once, yes, far to the east. There, against a wooden fortress."

"Fortress, boat, wood is wood. It does seem the loss of good arrows. Still"—a sharp shrug—"we shall do it."

The Medjai had kindled a fire—carefully screened, since they hardly wished to set the *Rising in Memphis* ablaze—and were dipping arrowheads wrapped in cloth into the flames till the cloth caught.

"Draw," Knife commanded, and a dozen bows were drawn, arrowheads blazing. "Aim. Release."

A dozen arrows flew straight to their target, the nearest ship, hitting in a dozen places. Most were extinguished on impact, but some took fire.

"Again," Knife repeated in that calm, clipped voice.

"Draw. Aim. Release. Ah," he added to Methos, "this is too easy."

"Enjoy the ease," Methos snapped back, staring at the Hyksos fleet. This was his idea; if it failed, the weight of that failure would be on his head.

Ha, but it was working! The targeted ship was fully ablaze, and of course the Hyksos ships were undermanned; no need to tie up whole crews in peacetime.

Another bad mistake.

By the time what sailors were aboard had started to cut the flaming ship free, the fire had jumped to the next ship, and the next. Methos could see frantic figures, dark against the flames, scurrying about, then giving up and diving overboard. The flames *might* keep the crocodiles at bay; the men *might* survive.

Kamose, laughing, unbent enough to slap Methos on the back in wild congratulation. "Clever, oh clever! No fleet for Apophis!"

"Clever, indeed," Prince Ahmose agreed, and seemed to almost mean it.

By now, alarm trumpets were sounding all over Avaris, the harsh calls echoing out over the Nile, frightening waterfowl into a storm of flapping wings.

And so, Methos thought, *with nothing more dramatic than this, the flight of a few ducks, the Battle of Avaris has begun.*

Chapter Twenty-three

Egypt, Avaris: Reigns of Pharaoh Kamose and King Apophis, 1570 B.C.

As the Egyptian ships neared the shore, the hastily assembled Hyksos warriors stood waiting in row after row for the enemy, looking grimly confident.

"They won't be expecting this," Kamose gloated. "They think us an untrained mob armed only with inferior weapons and no armor."

Methos raised an eyebrow. "The element of surprise doesn't last very long."

"Long enough. Knife?"

"We are within range, oh pharaoh."

"Then begin!"

"As the pharaoh wishes. Draw," Knife told his Medjai calmly. "Aim. Release. Yes. Repeat."

The Medjai had, in the proper way, aimed their shots high so that even an arrow that overshot the first row might well strike a man in the second or third, a warrior who'd, till the final instant, considered himself safe. On shore, men begun crying out as arrows struck true and men began falling, dying.

"Now!" Kamose shouted.

Under cover of the archers' continuing fire, the Egyptians rushed ashore, swords drawn, shouting savage war cries that blurred into one great mass of noise. The Hyksos warriors were silent, braced, the security of the walls to their backs. Frantic Hyksos archers up in the watchtowers and on the walls were finally bringing their own bows into play, but it was already too late. They couldn't fire without hitting their own men, and the two forces clashed, sword against sword.

Methos, who had fully intended to stay out of things, safely back with the Medjai, found himself instead caught in the crush, swept forward despite himself (or perhaps because of himself?), straight into the heart of the battle.

And realized with a sudden blaze of unexpected fury as he closed with the Hyksos, with those who had watched Nebet's death that *yes,* as he slashed across a foe's throat, dodging the gush of blood, he did wish this fight after all, and *yes,* as he sent another foe crumpling, screaming, he still wanted blood for Nebet, he still wanted vengeance for her death, he still wanted—

Another Immortal! The sudden warning shocked Methos into momentary calm, and he drew back, panting, the shouts and screams and reek of battle all about him, hunting the one he knew must be nearby:

Khyan! Yes, there he was in the crush, fighting like a demon, eyes flaming with bloodlust. Methos, once again just as savage, gladly began to cut his way through the enemy, heading blindly toward—

No! Gods, no! Sanity stabbed at him again, sharp and cold as a blade. *Are you utterly insane? What if he gets you?* No guarantee of taking a head, not in this crush. *And anyone suddenly resurrecting in the middle of battle is going to be just as suddenly beheaded as a demon!*

His moment of hesitation nearly got him killed. A surge of bodies crashed against Methos, sending him staggering off his feet, tumbling him right into the canal. Pjedku Canal, his mind provided inanely, and wonderful, he thought wildly, he knew the name of where he was about to die—and die he would, because a Hyksos warrior had just fallen on him, stronger than he, forcing his head under the water's surface no matter how fiercely he struggled. Once he was drowned, he'd probably die for good; the warrior would probably take himself a bloody souvenir, a nice new head to add to the Hyksos collection. But with the air running out, there didn't seem to be anything Methos could do about stopping him.

Without warning, the pressure was suddenly gone. Methos burst to the surface, gasping and choking, coughing his lungs clear, just in time to see Ahmose-the-Soldier run the Hyksos warrior through, then neatly slash a trophy hand off the body.

"You all right?" the young man panted, grinning, clutching his bloody trophy in triumph.

Methos managed a nod, then struggled soggily back to land, finding and snatching up his sword again. He lost sight of Ahmose-the-Solider in the next wave of warriors, and concentrated only on one thing: surviving, working his way back in slow, bloody stages to the relative safety of the ships. Nothing like almost getting drowned to shake the battle fury out of a man.

Who was it first called retreat? Methos could have sworn he'd suddenly heard it simultaneously in both Egyptian and Hyksos—yes, the Hyksos were in full retreat, swarming back into their fortress, and the heavy gates were inexorably closing.

Those last few Hyksos caught outside after the gates shut turned on the approaching Egyptians with grim resignation, knowing that they faced their deaths. But a storm of arrows from the walls drove the Egyptians back across the torn, bloody field to the relative safety at the water's edge, just out of bowshot. The gate opened barely a man's width, and most of the trapped Hyksos scrambled back into the fortress before the gate slammed shut with harsh finality.

Into the fortress, Methos thought, *where they will die more slowly.*

He was all at once aware of his immediate surroundings, seeing that he stood next to Knife, who shrugged at him. "That," the Medjai leader said fatalistically, "is that. We do not so easily breach those walls."

"And they," Methos retorted, wiping sweat and blood off his face with a hand that he only realized now was shaking with weariness, "do not so easily visit us again. We have a powerful ally in there."

"Eh?"

"Thirst, Knife. Our ally now is the demon thirst."

He saw Knife's white teeth flash in his sharp grin. "Ah, and a fine, strong demon that is, too! Let him play his games, and we shall see what we shall see."

Prince Ahmose, trailing frantic guards, hurried down from the *Rising in Memphis,* clearly furious at not having been allowed to fight. "Now what?" he asked.

"Now," Methos and Knife said almost as one, "we wait."

A day into the Siege of Avaris brought nothing much. The Egyptian priest-physicians, their linen robes no longer spotless, tended the wounded and, in their spare moments, cast spells against the Hyksos.

Spells, Methos thought dourly. *I have yet to see the magic that could bring down so much as a brick from a wall.*

Still, anything that gave the Egyptian warriors hope was a good thing.

Meanwhile, Ahmose-the-Soldier dared the Pjedku Canal again to pick off one of the Hyksos stragglers and gain himself another hand and a second Gold of Valor ornament. Knife and his Medjai scavenged the battlefield, one eye warily on the watchtowers, gathering what arrows they safely could find.

And everyone else . . . waited.

They were still waiting a day later. There was, Methos realized, no word for "siege" in the Egyptian language, though he suspected that there soon would be. If and when this one succeeded.

The fishing boats that had joined the royal flotilla were turning out to be very convenient, adding to the royal ships to create a total blockade of Avaris. Under cover of the

Medjai, warriors had dragged the bodies of the fallen off the field, burying the Egyptian dead as best they could to the accompanying murmurings of the priests, dumping the Hyksos casualties into the Nile for the crocodiles with no ceremony at all. No risk of plague either way, Methos thought approvingly.

Around him, men were making themselves as comfortable as possible on the dank ground. Someone had brought dice, and Methos could hear the faint rattling and muttered wagering. Someone else manufactured a makeshift flute out of a reed and played the same shrill tune on it over and over till it was snatched from his hand.

I'll take dankness and even the torment of a truly untalented flutist over a lack of water. I don't know how full their water tanks are in there, but a man needs a fair amount of liquid each day in this climate. The Siege of Avaris can't last too much longer. All we truly need out here is patience.

Unfortunately, Pharaoh Kamose seemed to be running out of that resource as quickly as the Hyksos must be running out of water within the walls. Pacing back and forth on the shore, he snapped, "This is ridiculous! They are not going to surrender, Methos, no matter what you say, no and we are caught here till—ha, look at those bastards up on the walls!"

What taunts they were hurling couldn't be heard at this range, but the obscene gestures were unmistakable.

"Knife!" Kamose commanded. "Shoot me those men!"

The Medjai archer cocked his head thoughtfully, measuring distance with a practiced eye. "Not possible, oh pharaoh," he said after a moment. "The distance, yes. But the wind is with them just now. They might shoot as far as this; but we as far as them, no."

"What nonsense is this? Give me a bow. Give me a bow, I told you!"

With a shrug, Knife gestured to one of his men, who reluctantly surrendered his bow. Kamose nocked an arrow, took a step forward, another, drew—

"No!" Methos shouted, a bare instant too late. As though

time had slowed, he saw the Hyksos archer on the walls shoot, the wind in his favor, saw the arrow flash through the air—saw Kamose fall. Methos and Knife rushed forward together, carrying the wounded pharaoh back to the safety of the water's edge, and were instantly surrounded by a mob of horrified Egyptians.

"Get back, idiots!" Methos snapped at them. "Give him room."

But then he saw the severity of the wound and silently amended that to *room in which to die*. That arrow had been far too accurately aimed.

Kamose knew it, too. "That," he gasped with the ghost of a smile, "was a damnably stupid thing to do." He broke off, coughing, and blood frothed on his lips. After a moment, he called weakly, "Ahmose . . . ?"

". . . brother . . . ?"

"Do better . . . than me. Be wiser. Free . . . our . . . Egypt." He slid into unconsciousness.

And that night, Pharaoh Kamose, son of the slain Pharaoh Sekenenre, joined his father among the gods.

Somewhere in the confusion that followed, Prince Ahmose managed to slip away. Methos found him in the shelter of the *Rising in Memphis's* hold, huddled in misery, and cleared his throat tactfully.

The boy looked sharply up at Methos's approach, his face wet. "What am I to do?"

It was, for this one last moment, the voice of a frightened child. Methos, moved by a tenderness he never would have expected in himself, knelt by the youngster's side, letting Ahmose cling to him, feeling the boy shake with sobs for his brother, for himself.

"I'm sorry," Methos said at last, drawing back. Hardening his voice, he added, "This is not the time for weakness."

The boy shuddered, then ran a brusque hand over his eyes, struggling for self-control. "No," he said. "I know. I . . . am pharaoh now, and I . . . I will rule. The Hyksos," he added with sudden coldness, "will pay and pay most dearly for this."

"So they shall," Methos agreed, just as coldly, aware that he no longer was in the presence of a boy. *And so Tetisheri's Gift proves true yet again.* "Pharaoh Ahmose, you must let your troops see you, know that you are alive and strong."

"Yes." The new pharaoh stood, fighting down his trembling till it was gone. "They shall know this. And so, to their eternal regret, shall the Hyksos."

Another day of seige. Kamose's body was preserved as best as was possible, utilizing every spare ounce of salt on all the ships and distilled from the Nile, tidal and drawing in the salt water from the sea at that point. A coterie of priests continually surrounded the body, praying without rest for the safety of the pharaoh's soul.

Meanwhile, life went on. Men fished in the river, hunted waterfowl on its banks, honed weapons, and tested bowstrings. All that was lacking in all this activity, Methos thought, was any sign of camaraderie.

How could there be any? They've lost their second ruler in three short years, and are left with an untested boy.

Not exactly a boy anymore. Ahmose did seem to be holding up remarkably well—so filled with anger toward the Hyksos, Methos mused, that he had no room left for grief or fear.

And the new pharaoh had, after all, been raised to lead. His finger stabbed at the most leather-lunged of his warriors. "You, you, and you: I want you to shout into the city, 'We have water, sweet water! Throw down your weapons and join us! Drink all you wish!' "

Two more days of siege. Two more days of shouting to the people of Avaris with no apparent effect.

Two more days, Methos thought, of wondering if he'd been right or wrong. Were they really desperate for water in there? What if there really was some hidden spring within Avaris, and he'd been too foolish, too overconfident, to find it? What if—

"The doors," someone snapped, and everyone came alert.

Sure enough, the massive gates of Avaris were creaking open.

"At last!" Ahmose cried in relief.

Every warrior stood rigidly on guard; every priest began murmuring protective prayers. This would be the final battle. They all knew it.

One way or another, only one ruler would be left alive when it was done.

Chapter Twenty-four

Egypt, Avaris: Reigns of Pharaoh Ahmose and King Apophis, 1570 B.C.

I never will learn, Methos thought, slashing, blocking, slashing, battling foe after foe, *never.*

But this *was* his fight now, as much as anyone's. He had sworn to bring down the Hyksos world, and by the gods, he was going to give it his best!

By now, though, his sword arm was aching. No, Methos corrected, his whole body was aching, bruised, cut, and stabbed a dozen times; the wounds, of course, none of them that serious, healed, but not as swiftly as he would have liked. And the accumulating shocks of pain reverberated up and down the nerves and mind long after the injury was gone, taking their toll.

Somewhere in this loud, bloody, reeking chaos, Khyan was also battling, no mistaking that, but the prince was hidden in the mob of warriors.

Mob, yes. The Hyksos were men downright maddened by thirst and the knowledge that the Nile was flowing so tantalizingly near—if only they could get past the barrier of the Egyptian warriors determined to stop them. Behind the Hyksos, trying frantically to push their way past, were the ordinary people of Avaris, desperate beyond the bonds of sanity, adding to the crush, trapping warriors of both sides in a press so tight they could not use their swords, trampling the fallen underfoot.

And Apophis—could that fierce, powerful figure, face half hidden by the leather, bronze-studded helmet, be the king himself, cutting his way brutally out through his own people? The king come to join in the fighting? If so, Methos thought with a jolt of hope, then the Hyksos truly were at the edge of despair, and the end would come soon.

The end for them, he corrected. *Nebet, I vowed the end of all their world—let it be so!*

His guard slipped during that instant of thought. Methos gasped, stumbling, nearly falling as unexpected new pain blazed through him, and the Hyksos warrior who'd just stabbed him laughed, sure of victory.

But the laugh froze on the mortal's face when Methos, secure in the knowledge that a mere stabbing couldn't be fatal, laughed savagely back at him. The mortal's mouth dropped open in horror as the victim he'd thought already dead parried what should have been the death blow. In the next moment, he was dead, throat cut open, and Methos, panting, covered with blood that wasn't all his, stood waiting for his wound to heal, glancing fiercely about for more foes to—

Apophis. He was looking straight at Apophis, the king's strong-featured face a mask of despairing rage.

The world seemed to freeze about them. There was only this, two men staring at each other in utter hatred

Then Methos took a step forward. "For Nebet," he said.

But Egyptian warriors were swarming over Apophis, tearing the sword from his hand, forcing him to his knees despite his furious struggles, and Methos heard himself cry out in cheated rage, "You can't! He's mine!"

No one heeded. Of course not! This was hardly the place for a personal feud, not when the king of the Hyksos was taken and the battle was won!

Not quite:

Khyan!

The prince came charging blindly forward to free his brother, cutting down two, three, five men who moved to stop him. Methos calmly raised his sword, sure that single combat was about to begin, like it or not, an Immortal duel to the death—

But there were too many Egyptians even for one utterly crazed Immortal to fight, and Khyan was dragged down, struggling with all the useless ferocity of a captured bull till he was forced prone.

With him went the last of the collective Hyksos heart. More and more of the warriors lowered their blades or threw them away, rushing past the Egyptians for the Nile, drinking and drinking, heedless of danger from men or crocodiles. The common folk came in the next rush, just like the soldiers seeing only the water, the precious, wonderful water.

"Let them drink," Pharaoh Ahmose ordered. "Our fight is not with them. It never was with them."

Some died, convulsing, from too much water taken too suddenly. Others lay in utter exhaustion or crept into kneeling submission. Soon there was silence on the field save for the moans and cries of the wounded.

Those cries ended, one by one: The Egyptians were in no mood for mercy save for their own, and saw no need for prisoners.

Save for the royal two. Apophis was dragged before the young pharaoh, fighting his captors, refusing to kneel.

"Let him be," Ahmose ordered.

He and the fierce-eyed Hyksos king studied each other, Ahmose looking even younger, almost fragile, against Apophis's powerful bulk.

But Methos saw that there was nothing at all youthful in Ahmose's eyes. "What am I to do with you?" the pharaoh wondered coolly.

"Kill me, damn you, *boy*. Kill me and let me haunt your dreams!"

"My dreams are my own. And boy I may be, but I am no fool. One thing I do not need is a royal martyr."

Ahmose's sharp glance took in Methos and the others, then focused on the Egyptian priests. "Advise me," he ordered them. "What shall be done with this one?"

The priests consulted, whispering among themselves, glancing at Apophis, at Ahmose. Methos felt Apophis's hot stare and turned to stare right back.

"Why?" the king snarled. "You are not one of them!"

Methos let himself smile a cold, thin, humorless smile. "Ah," he purred, "but Nebet was."

Blankness. Of course: A king would hardly need to remember the name of a slave.

"Nebet," Methos continued, his voice still a purr, "whom you forced me to destroy. Nebet, whose only sin was loving me."

"Ah, that one! The little scar-faced slut! I never thought you were so—"

"For shame, Apophis." Methos kept his voice pitched at that same deadly softness. "I am not that weak. No matter how you beg, I won't give you an easy death."

Khyan couldn't have heard too much of that, but he suddenly convulsed under the men holding him captive, nearly tearing free, shouting out foulnesses at Methos in the Hyksos tongue, insane curses that made no sense.

Coldly, Methos turned back to Ahmose and the cluster of priests. The chief among them, the priest of Amun, a tall, lean man of indeterminate age and great dignity, dipped his head in grave courtesy to Ahmose.

"We have decided, oh pharaoh. This is, enemy or no, a king. He cannot be slain like a common man."

"No," Ahmose agreed reluctantly. "How, then?"

Let me, Methos thought. *Ah, let me.* "I have witnessed the rites of Set," he cut in. "It seems only just that he should, in turn—"

Cries of horror, denial, from the priests interrupted him: They were civilized men! They would not sink to such depths!

Unless it suited you.

"Besides," the priest of Amun added thoughtfully, "he is, as you remind us, a royal follower of Set. And as such, his soul is far too perilous to release. It would fly straight to that god to tell Set what we have done. That we cannot risk. Instead . . ."

With a lunge swift as the striking of a snake, the priest snatched up Apophis's fallen sword.

"Hear us, oh men of Egypt, men of the Hyksos: Apophis, once known as King of Avaris, will meet this fate. His body will be slain, smothered so that his royal blood will not be shed—but his soul will be trapped forever in this, his own sword!"

"Nooo!" Khyan wailed in horrified pain. "Brother, nooo!"

As warriors folded robes over Apophis's nose and mouth, holding him helpless for all the ferocity of his struggles, the priests began their chanting.

"Hail to thee, Osiris, Lord of Eternity.
Hail to thee, oh King of the Gods.
Let him not pass."

"Stop it!" Khyan screamed. "Stop it!"
But the priests' voices never wavered.

"Hail to the first Doorkeeper, Sekhet.
Let him not pass.
Hail to the second Doorkeeper, Unhat.
Let him not pass."

Superstition, Methos thought. *No matter how a mortal dies, death still holds the same permanence.*

But the slightest of, yes, superstitious pricklings raced up his spine, regardless.

And the priests continued relentlessly as Apophis fought with all the desperate strength in his body, as the warriors pressed the robes more firmly over his nose and mouth:

"Hail to the sixth Doorkeeper, Atek.
Let him not pass.
Hail to the seventh Doorkeeper, Sekmet.

Let him not pass."

Khyan twisted his head free of those who were trying to silence him. "Brother! My brother! No, fight them, live! No!"

But Apophis's frenzied fight for life was starting to lessen. And the priests chanted on:

"Let this soul be blocked.
Let it not pass.
Let this soul be trapped.
Through all the eons,
Let it be trapped.
Through all the eons,
Let it never know rest,
Let it never know peace,
Let it never know life."

Apophis's struggle slowed . . . slowed . . . stopped. The warriors warily released their holds, and the royal body crumpled, lifeless.

"Brother!"

It was a shout of wildest agony. Twisting about to stare at Methos, Khyan screamed, "You! Demon! It is your doing, all this, all the wrongness, all your doing! *Demon!* Yes, hear me, this is no man but a *demon!* Cut him—and see him heal!"

"He is insane," Methos began.

But with a surge of that insane strength and speed, Khyan was free, snatching a sword and lunging. Methos felt the blade like an icy blaze through his chest, and had time only to think, *Not here, not now.* Choking, he tried to cry out, "Damn you."

But it was too late for words.

And then, with the usual stunning suddenness, there was light and life again, and he was coughing his lungs clear, struggling to breathe, struggling to regain his feet and dazed senses. Khyan had been caught by the others, which was, Methos realized, the only reason he was coming back to life at all.

Absolute silence fell, everyone staring at Methos. They had all seen him die. He couldn't possibly pretend it had been nothing but a trick.

"Impossible," someone breathed. And, "A miracle," others gasped.

But it was Ahmose who shouted out, eyes cold, "Demon! This is no 'man sent by the gods'—this was never a man at all, but a betrayer of men! *Demon!*"

There was no doubt at all that he knew exactly what he said, without the slightest trace of superstition. And of course, since the pharaoh had said it, the others were echoing, "Demon! Demon!"

There's gratitude for you!

Or was it that the clever Ahmose didn't want another clever man around? One who just might be too ambitious a man? One who had seen the boy god-king in his all too-human weakness? No matter: The sudden betrayal hurt Methos more than he ever would have credited.

Never mind, never mind, just get out of here before anything else goes wrong!

Which it did: Khyan tore free once more and attacked.

All right, then, Methos thought in despair, *let them see a Quickening!*

His sword clashed against Khyan's stolen blade, once, twice—

Then Medjai arrows cut short the fight. Methos felt agony blaze through him, felt himself convulse with the impact, crying out, at the same time hearing Khyan's scream.

The prince fell, dying, pierced by half a dozen arrows. But with one last effort, he forced himself up on an elbow, shouting out, "I curse you, Ahmose, curse you with all my might! I will free my brother's soul, I swear this, *though it take me the lifetime of the world!*"

For that one shocked moment, all attention was focused on the prince. "Get out of here," someone whispered violently shoving Methos: Ahmose-the-Soldier, eyes wild with his own daring. "Don't know what you are; don't want to know. But you're a brave fighter. Go on!"

The Egyptian turned on the others, pointing at the fallen Khyan, yelling, "Demon! There's the demon! Come on, stone him!"

The strategy was thinner than papyrus, but in that moment of mob hysteria, Methos, biting his lip till it bled against the pain, concentrated only on surviving, only on moving, step by unsteady step, to the river's edge. He would not collapse. He would not give up, no matter how his agonized body was failing him. He was not going to die here, damn them all, not going to lose his head to those he'd thought friends.

A way out . . . must be a way . . .

Yes, yes, one of the fishing boats, little thing . . . no one on board . . .

Methos fell into it, helplessly crying out at the blinding new slash of pain. Darkness swirled before his eyes—no, no, he could not die, not yet!

Gasping, nearly sobbing in his agony, he slashed the anchor rope, let the sail unfurl. The wind caught it, pulling the rope from his hands, filling the sail . . . sweetest sight in the world . . . sail like the belly of a pregnant woman . . . couldn't remember who'd said that . . .

It didn't matter. As the little boat sped over the Nile, Methos fell helplessly back onto the deck, dimly aware he'd passed beyond the point of pain, dimly aware of the breath rasping in his lungs growing slower . . . ever slower. He lay staring up at the clear, beautiful turquoise-blue desert sky . . .

. . . and then . . .

Darkness.

Chapter Twenty-five

New York City, Midtown:
The Present

"If I can make it there, I'll make it anywhere . . ."
The lines from that more or less anthem of New York City, "New York, New York," insisted on running through Duncan MacLeod's mind as he hung from the balcony in the Branson Collection there in the middle of the night.

It certainly was true, at least, that you could find anything you needed in this city—including the rope and tackle from which he was suspended right now. That had come, no questions asked, as part of rock-climbing gear, from a sporting goods store over on Third Avenue, as had the soft-sided case, meant for a tennis racket, that should be just the right size to hold the Hyksos sword, and the narrow-beam, tight-focus flashlight that was letting him see where he was going without lighting up the whole gallery. A hardware store next door had provided an archaic but functioning walkie-talkie set, of which he had one half and Methos the other, and a nice, compact tool kit holding a pair of wire cutters, pliers, and screwdriver.

Methos, up on the Branson balcony, having won or lost the toss of the coin (depending on how one felt about rope climbing), was watching him intently, a dimly seen figure up there, face ghostly pale. MacLeod nodded, *I'm all right,* and began his wary hand-over-hand climb down the nicely knotted rope. He didn't *think* the Branson

Collection had alarmed the floor as well as the doorways, but there was no reason to take unnecessary risks.

As opposed to necessary ones? This is not the way I like spending an evening.

Outside, the night was rapidly turning nasty, building up to what promised to be a truly Gothic storm.

Just what we need. Or rather, don't need.

A preliminary flash of lightning made him start, nearly losing his hold on the rope and making it swing alarmingly as he clung to it. MacLeod caught a flash of Methos's face, eyes wide with apprehension.

Not much I can do. Just wait till I stop swinging . . . ah, there.

It had been ridiculously easy to break into the Branson Collection. He and Methos had merely hid in a supply closet till the building had been shut for the night.

Good thing we're not trying to rob a larger museum.

He wouldn't have cared to tackle something, say, the size and sophistication of the Metropolitan Museum of Art, not without Amanda's help.

To be fair, security was perfectly tight in the Branson Foundation offices, where vital data were kept. But it was, by comparison, on the casual side out here in the galleries, where the one guard had gone off on a coffee break. Who, after all, was going to break into an exhibit containing nothing of flashy worth?

Only a four-hundred-year-old Scottish Highlander and a . . . who-knows-how-old whatever-he-is.

Of course, a coffee break only lasted so long. No time to waste, unless he *wanted* to explain to Professor Maxwell why he was here after closing hours.

At least the coming storm, rumbling its way toward the city, should drown out any noise he might make. It should be reasonably easy to get out of here again, too. Go back up the rope, then out and down the side of the elaborately ornate building. All those nice stone handholds.

Hopefully not slick with rain by that point.

The sword in its case was right below him. Fortunate

that said case was one of the old-fashioned, plain-glass-box-in-wood-frame variety. He wasn't sure he could have opened a more modern version, but this . . . well, now, MacLeod knew he'd never admit to Amanda just how much he'd learned from her.

There must be an alarm wire, though . . . yes, there it was, a nice, simple one, too. A quick clip with the wire cutters took care of it. Some delicate work with pliers and screwdriver, and . . . ha, yes, that did it.

Hanging from the rope by one foot braced in a knotted loop, MacLeod gingerly raised the glass lid of the case. One slip and . . .

But he didn't slip, and no, the case had no secret alarms, either. Unless they were silent?

No might-be's!"

MacLeod gently lifted the Hyksos sword free of its stand and slipped it into the tennis racket case slung across his chest—ha, yes, a perfect fit. He just as carefully closed the museum case, then started his careful way back up the rope, hand over hand, to rejoin Methos. Giving up the tennis racket case with a flourish, MacLeod told him, "All yours."

Methos gave a curt nod. "Now to see if our trap catches its prey."

"Well," MacLeod said with forced good cheer, "you know where I'll be. Happy hunting!"

"Did anyone ever tell you, MacLeod, that you have a very bizarre sense of humor?"

Methos was gone into the shadows before MacLeod could reply.

MacLeod winced at the sound of thunder and fought the urge to glance up yet again. He knew what was up there: clouds. Dark, heavy, threatening clouds. The storm would be upon them soon enough, and at least he could take some consolation in the fact that it wasn't raining.

Yet.

The wind was rising, chilly for mid-May. MacLeod

pulled the collar of his trenchcoat up about his ears and continued his prowl on the sidewalk surrounding the Branson Collection. Fifth Avenue—Seventy-first Street—Madison Avenue—Seventieth Street—back to Fifth Avenue, hand never that far from the hilt of his concealed sword, and never mind that the square of land he was covering was too large for him to sense Khyan if Khyan happened to be on the far side of the building. Methos and he had already agreed that it was impossible for any one man to keep watch over an entire building. All MacLeod could do was keep up this constant quadrangular stalk, hoping some overzealous policeman wasn't keeping tabs on this eccentric walker, and wait for the warning of another Immortal's presence.

When. And if.

Another thing on which he and Methos had flatly agreed was that this was no place for heroics. Whichever one of them first spotted Khyan took care of him as quickly as possible.

Glaring at the streetlights, MacLeod added to himself, *Presuming that we can find some less brightly lit place. "See Immortals Fight to the Death Under a Spotlight!"*

Even if he couldn't get near enough to Khyan to stop him, MacLeod reminded himself, he would at least be able to warn Methos through their walkie-talkies.

One way or another, this ends tonight.

Assuming, of course, that Khyan shows up at all.

The weather, Methos thought, crouching on the roof of the Branson Collection and hoping no one on the surrounding building was going to look down and see him (though, he thought, they'd have needed a floodlight for that), was hardly cooperating.

At least it isn't raining. Yet.

He had to admit, though, that the great black clouds and the occasional flashes of lightning, thunder echoing and reechoing down the city canyon, certainly set the proper mood.

I already did my Gothic period, thank you very much.

MacLeod was, by now, somewhere back down on the sidewalk, staking out the outside of the museum. It would have been impossible for one man, even someone as efficient as Duncan, to keep watch over an entire building, so Methos and he had agreed that the first to catch any sense of another Immortal's approach would warn the other.

Assuming that there is such an approach. Assuming that this works and I'm not up here in the open during a thunderstorm, being a perfect target for lightning for nothing.

The sooner begun, the sooner done. Removing the sword from its makeshift case, Methos set it down before him and began his chant to show the "captured soul" he was its master.

I had forgotten just how different that era's beliefs were. I had forgotten so much . . .

Nebet. Poor, loving, doomed Nebet. He could, after so many centuries, remember only the faintest shadow of the passion he'd felt for her. He must have genuinely loved her, though; in fact, considering, Methos was sure of it. Why else would he have risked his neck for her? Why else make that utterly ridiculous vow about bringing down the entire Hyksos world?

It would have fallen without any help from me. And Khyan—yes, Khyan would still have survived, then till now, and would still be posing a threat.

And yes, I would probably still be trying to draw him here.

What had made him visit the Hyksos exhibit at all? There had been more than mere curiosity to the decision. Duncan, being Duncan, seemed to think it had all been part of an elaborate plot.

No. Not really. Not quite.

And yet . . . had he, deep within him, suspected that Khyan still lived?

Not suspected, Methos corrected, so much as guessed.

Not so much plotted, for that matter, as wanted to bring closure to a distant part of his life.

I'm getting as superstitious and maudlin as—as someone still living back in the once-upon-a-time. Which I most certainly am not.

On with the show.

MacLeod froze on Fifth Avenue, feeling . . . yes. Another Immortal was nearby.

And he has to be aware of me, too.

He hurried around the corner onto Seventy-first Street, to see a tall, shadowy figure tense, head up, looking this way and that, trying to locate the enemy.

That has to be Khyan!

Just then, a second, smaller man nearly collided with Khyan, presumably apologized, then began unlocking a door into the Branson Collection—

Khyan grabbed him, prodding his captive.

Something about that smaller figure . . . *Professor Maxwell!* MacLeod realized, racing forward.

Khyan all but hurled his captive inside. MacLeod was just in time to have the door slammed in his face.

Damn, damn, damn!

But Khyan had been in too much of a hurry. The door hadn't fully latched, and MacLeod hurled it open—only to be confronted by a wall of nearly total darkness: The other Immortal wasn't risking letting Maxwell turn on any lights.

But they'd have to have *some* way to see where they were going—

There! The thinnest trace of light meant Khyan or Maxwell had a flashlight. Moving smoothly up—an elevator! They could only be heading up to the roof. MacLeod took a rashly hasty step forward and nearly fell over a body just inside the doorway: a security guard, a hand told him, uniform sticky with blood and throat quickly cut by Khyan.

Have to warn Methos!

He wasn't sure the archaic walkie-talkie would work indoors. MacLeod stuck his head back outside, whispering, "He's on his way." That would have to be good enough, he thought; no time for more. Light from outside shone through the open doorway, glinting off—ha, yes, those were the marble steps of a stairway leading up. MacLeod ducked back inside, letting the door close behind him, sprinted over the body, and dashed up the stairs as quickly as he could in the once-again total darkness. He wasn't going to get to the roof before Khyan—

But damned if I'm going to let Maxwell die.
Be ready for us, Methos, just be ready!

"Oh soul of a king, hear me, heed me, fear me.
Oh soul of a king, I rule you, control you, torment you . . ."

Gesturing and chanting with all his might, Methos thought dryly that he was, indeed, putting on quite a show. Some of the chant was in genuine Hyksos and Egyptian, but most of it was made up as he went along: It really had been a *long* time since he'd spoken either language.

"Oh soul of a king, oh soul of a foe, heed me!
Oh soul of a king, you are my slave!"

Is this going to work? Am I making a fool of myself for nothing?
Ha, do I even want *it to work?*
"Oh soul of a king—"
The sudden sharp crackle of static cut through his words. Snatching up the walkie-talkie, Methos heard "He's on his way."
Want it or not, the paper trail and "ritual" were working. Methos braced himself, heart racing. In another moment he, too, was going to be sensing Khyan's presence.

And with any luck at all, MacLeod and he would have Khyan trapped between them.

So they did. Unfortunately, Methos saw at once, it wasn't exactly as they'd planned. Yes, he felt the sudden familiar blaze of warning. And yes, that was definitely Khyan who had just appeared out of the night, framed melodramatically by flashes of lightning. Dressed as he was in modern American clothing, the former Hyksos prince could have been any Near Eastern young man.

Any Near Eastern man, that was, who happened to have utterly mad, blazing eyes, a gleaming sword in one hand—and a small, slight man caught as a hostage in the other. Some curatorial staffer, presumably, who had picked a really bad night to work late!

No, Methos realized in the next moment, the hostage was none other than Professor Albert Maxwell himself, babbling frantically and incoherently in English and Arabic at his captor, who was ignoring him.

Does Maxwell recognize me? Methos wondered with a flash of alarm. *No. The night's too dark. And after all, he's only seen me once before.*

And did Khyan recognize Methos? No telling: That savage, fierce-eyed face showed no comprehensible emotions at all.

"Give me the sword." Khyan's voice was harsh, heavy with a miscellaneous tangle of accents and a wildness that was barely being formed into words. The blazing eyes stared, unblinking as those of a snake and still showing no sign of recognition, straight at Methos. "Give me the sword, or I will kill this man."

Insanity beyond anything he's ever shown before, Methos thought. And despite all he had seen in his life, all he had done, he felt a chill of genuine horror steal through him. *Utter, utter insanity.*

For here was every Immortal survivor's nightmare brought to life: the total loss of self. It was difficult enough for Methos to hold fast to what he was at the heart of him, to the basic "Methos," after all the years and experiences. But this . . . While the body he faced still lived, nothing at all was left of the true Khyan, not judging from those terrible, empty eyes, nothing after so many centuries of madness but the unbreakable will to find and free his brother's soul.

One good thing about it: Khyan was definitely too far gone to realize the trap. Not by the slightest twitch of a muscle did Methos betray that MacLeod had appeared on the roof, too, and was circling around behind Khyan.

Unfortunately, Maxwell was far too terrified for common sense. "Help me!" he yelped at MacLeod. "In God's name, help me!"

Khyan whirled, dragging his captive around with him, and Methos, knowing he'd only have a bare second's advantage, lunged with the weapon at hand—not his own sword, he realized a heartbeat too late, but the Hyksos blade.

Warned by some insane instinct, Khyan twisted about again, dodging. He lost his grip on Maxwell, who went flying and then scrambled up and wisely scurried away without so much as a glance back.

Khyan never noticed. Lightning blazed off the length of his blade as he attacked, shrieking out something that might have been his name, slashing at Methos again and again with a graceful, deadly savagery, never giving Methos so much as a second's respite in which to draw his own sword.

Wonderful, wonderful, I've got a three-thousand-year-old weapon, worn-out bronze, barely an edge—

He caught a glimpse of MacLeod's alarmed face, but damn it, of course Duncan couldn't interfere, not in a duel between Immortals.

Does he have to play so utterly by the rules? Of course he does; he's Duncan MacLeod. Methos dodged, slipped, landed on one knee with a jarring thump. *But I haven't lived this long by being stupid!*

There was always grit on any Manhattan rooftop, and a hastily thrown handful hit Khyan full in his eyes. As the

Hyksos clawed fiercely at his vision, screaming his rage, Methos quickly backed up out of range—only to have his escape blocked with a jolt by the stone parapet rimming the roof, and here came the lunatic charging blindly forward, about to spit him—

"Wait!" Lying frantically, Methos warned, "Break this sword, and your brother's soul dies forever!"

Khyan stopped short, just barely in time, so frantically he actually staggered back a few steps, giving Methos, finally, the chance to draw his own sword, awkwardly juggling the Hyksos sword, transferring it to his own left hand, since he dared not put it down and risk Khyan getting it. In another second—

To Methos's shock, the prince threw back his head with a keen of anguish. So horrifying was the sound, so utterly inhuman, that Methos, for all his peril, stood frozen. In that primal instant, the centuries slid rapidly away; in that primal instant, he was not of the twentieth century, the modern age, but a man of an ancient, ancient time, when "natural" and "supernatural" were one and the same. And it hardly seemed surprising that the heavens should open and rain come pouring down as though in answer to Khyan's wild grief.

"All these years," Khyan shrilled, "all the long, long empty years have I kept the faith!" His words were a hodgepodge of English, Arabic, Hyksos, all the languages he'd learned in whatever snatches of sanity had been his. "All the long, empty, miserable years have I hunted for my brother's soul! All these years—no longer! I will not let my brother suffer anymore!"

Methos came crashing back into the twentieth century as Khyan charged him. Their swords clashed, the shock of impact nearly staggering Methos. He'd always said an ignorant swordsman was far more dangerous than an expert, being less predictable or sensible of peril—now he could add "insane" to "ignorant." Nothing ignorant here, but nothing predictable, either, no pattern to Khyan's thrusts or cuts or lunges, and Methos was getting cut far too often without being able to figure out his opponent's mad style.

"Watch the eyes," the swordsman's wisdom went. "You can predict his next move from his eyes."

Oh, right! *Nothing in there but chaos.*

He decided to try a little madness of his own. Lunge like this, like this, drive Khyan back at least a few stumbling steps, open up some space between them.

But Khyan, twisting like a snake, dodged, ducked, caught Methos's sword in one hand, never mind that the edge was cutting him to the bone. Methos did his own frantic twisting, nearly wrenching every muscle in the effort not to lose his weapon, flailing with his left hand to slam Khyan across the side of the head with the Hyksos sword. Not as hard as he'd have liked, not at that awkward angle, but at least Khyan had to let go of the trapped blade—

No predicting a madman. With a roar, Khyan threw himself at Methos, hurling him back with such stunning force that Methos banged his head painfully against the stone parapet. He held grimly onto his sword's hilt—but Khyan tore the Hyksos sword free and leaped up onto the parapet.

No, you don't, damn you! You don't escape this time!

That meant leaping up onto the parapet himself, even though he was still dizzy from that slam on the head, even though the cursed stone was slick with rain and alarmingly narrow, dueling with a madman who had the proverbial madman's strength.

A three-story drop—I hate this, hate it! Can't see where I'm stepping, can't lunge, can't retreat. Death by falling—hate the whole idea! If we both go over the edge and he recovers first—

All right, be just as insane. Lunge—yes! Hook Khyan's sword with his own, twist, yes! He tore the hilt from Khyan's hand and sent the blade flying who knew, and who cared where.

Off balance, sure he was falling, Methos hurled himself at Khyan: Take the enemy with him. For a mindless few moments, they grappled together, Khyan doing his best to get both hands around Methos's throat. Choking, Methos bit down on the nearest target, Khyan's arm, so hard that he tasted coppery blood, trying not to gag. Khyan tore himself free with a shriek—

And went hurtling backward off the parapet. Methos almost followed, struggling frantically to catch his balance. MacLeod's hand closed about his arm just in time, dragging him, panting and shaking, back onto the roof. No chance, though, to give MacLeod more than the briefest of nods.

Not the end of this, Methos thought breathlessly, *of course not the end of this.*

He and MacLeod exchanged quick, understanding glances, then raced down the Collection's stairs, out onto the now rain-slick sidewalk after Khyan.

Methos got there first, part of his mind thinking sardonically that now that the worst of it was over, he finally had the chance to use his sword sanely.

Well, maybe not quite the worst of it. Duncan MacLeod, being the ridiculously honorable man he was, might have waited for Khyan to recover.

I am not Duncan MacLeod.

Even so, Methos hesitated over the limp (but of course not finally dead) body for the barest instant, surprising himself by realizing that he was saying a final farewell to a long-ago time, and perhaps to a long-lost self.

What, he thought wildly, *sentiment after all these years?* and struck. He caught a quick glimpse of MacLeod staring at him—

And then the full effect of the Quickening hit him, the savage blaze and impact of being, of life-force, of sheer, wild insanity, and for a time out of time, Methos was lost in the familiar fierceness that was not-pain, not-pleasure. He was himself, he was Khyan, seeing so many faces, so many times and places. For those wild, wild moments he was all the ones he'd known, all those he'd slain over all the millennia, over all the long, long years of life and experience, of joy, grief, despair, passion, and it was almost too much, almost beyond all bearing. . . .

And in the last moment of it, he saw, or thought he saw, two figures of light merging into one, then fading into the night. Khyan and Apophis reunited?

Then, mercifully, it was over.

Methos was dimly aware of having fallen to his knees, but right now all he could do was huddle there in the pouring rain, too drained to move, testing out his mind the cautious way a warrior might warily probe at a wound to see if it was healed, half afraid of pain, trying to see if he was once more a single, whole, sane Methos. And he was truly glad in that helpless moment of reintegration of self that MacLeod was far too honorable for treachery.

And life wins out over death yet again. And . . . surprise, surprise, I do want to go on living after all.

But something was wrong. All about him, the fierce flashes of light and savage roar were continuing unquenched, along with a blaring, ear-hurting wail—

The flashes, he realized in the next instant, were merely lightning, the roar merely the noise of the storm. And that wailing? Car alarms, triggered by the force of the Quickening. A quick glance about showed a good many store windows cracked or downright shattered.

Oh joy. At least the Quickening would have been disguised: "Helluva storm we're having," and all that. Bet there are reports of a lightning strike in the area.

At last Methos could get shakily back to his feet—to find that MacLeod was watching him oddly.

"What?" Methos asked.

"Ah, nothing."

"What?" he insisted.

Reluctantly, MacLeod asked, "Did you see, just for an instant . . ."

There was a pause.

Then Methos shrugged, a little too enthusiastically. "A

trick of the light." He shivered, sneezed. "Let's go get ourselves a nice, peaceful drink."

"Excellent idea."

Together, the two men walked off into the night.

Afterword

In the modern story: New York City is as accurately portrayed as this New Yorker dared make it. However, just because the Branson Collection may occupy the same space as the Frick Collection, it is not to be confused with the Frick Collection, nor, to the best of the author's knowledge, is there actually a Branson Foundation!

As for the past story: Although time has been a bit telescoped for purposes of that story (and consistency with the Highlander timetable), the Hyksos really did invade and conquer Egypt circa 1700 B.C., though experts still argue as to whether it was a gradual invasion or one concerted attack, and they really were expelled after a hundred years of occupation, mostly through the efforts of Pharaohs Kamose and Ahmose, somewhere between 1600 and 1560 B.C.

The Hyksos were almost certainly a branch of the Canaanite people from Palestine, though little else is known about them. There is as yet no evidence as to whether or not they had a written language. They may or may not have been dictatorial toward the conquered; the view of them given in this book is very much from the Egyptian side, and the accounts of freedom fighters are seldom charitable toward those they consider oppressors!

Did the Hyksos rituals worshiping Set really involve human sacrifice and dismemberment? There's no evidence one way or the other. But since Set was said not only to have slain his brother Osiris but to have dismembered the body, it seemed a plausible extrapolation.

As for the settings: Memphis really had been sacked by the Hyksos to the point of near destruction, Thebes had not yet risen to prominence as the powerful capital of Egypt, and Nefrusy really was nearly razed by a furious Pharaoh Kamose. The description of Avaris, the Hyksos stronghold, is taken from the recent excavation reports of Professor Manfred Bietak.

Many of the characters in this book are historical, and are listed below in order of appearance:

Pharaoh Sekenenre really did die in battle, presumably against the Hyksos; his hastily embalmed mummy still shows his death wounds and dying grimace.

Pharaoh Kamose, his older son, reigned for only about three years. It's assumed that he, too, died of battle wounds; there's some evidence that he didn't live long enough to take part in the siege of Avaris. Most of his speeches in the book are taken from his actual words.

Pharaoh Ahmose, Kamose's younger brother, or possibly half-brother, did succeed to the throne at a very young age, either as a teen or (some evidence indicates) possibly even as a preteen. He grew into a strong ruler who expelled the last of the Hyksos, beat back the Nubians, and brought Egypt back to prominence as an independent power.

Dowager Queen Teti-sheri, grandmother of Ahmose (and possibly Kamose), was a lovely, delicate-featured woman, judging from the one surviving statue of her, a commoner who caught the eye of a pharaoh and who survived into her seventies or eighties. There is no evidence that she had any psychic abilities—but then again, there's no evidence that she had none!

Queen Ahhotep, of mixed Egyptian and Minoan blood, never appears onstage in this book, but was every bit as strong a personage as is implied in the story: She held the south of Egypt safe from Nubian attack, and possibly also served as regent for a time for Pharaoh Ahmose. She was remembered by him in an inscription honoring her for her help to him and Egypt.

King Apophis—who, according to the Egyptian accounts, did send that insulting message to Sekenenre—about the Roaring hippos—was, indeed, defeated at the Siege of Avaris, where he presumably was slain. We know nothing about his appearance or personality, other than that he was said to be a worshiper of Set, to the exclusion of any other deities.

The Ahmose referred to in this book as Ahmose-the-Soldier was a commoner, a career soldier who rose through the ranks all the way to admiral. It was the fashion in his day for the famous or well-to-do to leave their autobiographies on the walls of their tombs, and it is from Admiral Ahmose that we have the only firsthand account of the battles against the Hyksos, in particular of the Siege of Avaris.

For those wanting to read more about the period, and on ancient Egypt in general, the following are relatively recent, easily attainable books:

Bietak, Manfred. *Avaris, the Capital of the Hyksos: Recent Excavations at Tell El-Dab'a.* London: British Museum Press, 1996.

Clayton, Peter A. *Chronicle of the Pharaohs: The Reign-by-Reign Record of the Rulers and Dynasties of Ancient Egypt.* London: Thames & Hudson, 1994.

Grimal, Nicholas. *A History of Ancient Egypt.* Oxford and Cambridge: Blackwell Publishers, Ltd., 1992.

Manetho. (The writing of) *Manetho.* Translated by W. G. Waddell. Cambridge: Harvard University Press, 1940.

Pritchard, James B. *The Ancient Near East, A New Anthology of Texts and Pictures,* Volume II. Princeton: Princeton University Press, 1975.

Quirke, Stephen. *Ancient Egyptian Religion.* London: British Museum Press, 1992.

Redford, Donald B. *Egypt, Canaan, and Israel in Ancient Times.* Princeton: Princeton University Press, 1992.